LEXILAND

Suzi Moore

LEXILAND

SIMON AND SCHUSTER

First published in Great britain in 2013 by Simon and Schuster UK Ltd
A CBS COMPANY

1 3 5 7 9 10 8 6 4 2

Simon & Schuster UK Ltd
1st Floor, 222 Gray's Inn Road
London
WC1X 8HB

Simon & Schuster Australia, Sydney

Simon & Schuster India, New Delhi

A CIP catalogue record for this book is available from the British Library.

PB ISBN: 978-0-85707-508-6
eBook ISBN: 978-0-85707-509-3

Printed and bound by CPI Group (UK) Ltd, Croydon, CR0 4YY

www.simonandschuster.co.uk
www.simonandschuster.com.au

For Mum and Dad, with love, Suzi x

1

My sister died on March the first which was really annoying because it was my birthday.

It was *our* birthday. Laura was my identical twin.

It happened very quickly and the doctor said, 'It didn't hurt.' I said, 'At least she got to open all her presents first.' Mum didn't think that was funny. I told her that I wasn't *trying* to be funny, but I thought that, if it had been me, if *I* had choked on a slice of birthday cake, if it had been *my* very last birthday *ever*, I would have *at least* liked to have opened my presents first.

But, that doesn't really matter now, because I don't like birthdays any more.

I don't like Christmas any more either. We've had one Christmas without Laura and my mum was miserable. She cries a lot now. My parents argue a lot and my little brother, Rory, talks to the wallpaper.

Sometimes, I hear my parents shouting late at night and once I heard my mum say, 'Emma [that's me by the way] looks so like Laura that some days I find it hard to look at her. Sometimes, I think I'm looking at a ghost.'

The morning after that I went into the bathroom and, using the sharpest pair of scissors I could find, I cut off all my hair. *All of it.* But I couldn't reach the back so I was left with two dark brown tufts. I thought they looked a bit like mouse ears, so with a black felt tip I drew a black nose and six whiskers on my face. I showed Rory and he laughed so loud that Mum came into the bathroom to see what we were doing.

MUM: Oh my God! What have you done?

I wriggled my nose and smiled.

ME: Squeak! Squeak!

Rory was still laughing.

RORY: I wanna be a mouse *too*, Mummy! Can I? Can I? Please?

But Mum just cried and cried.

ME: What's wrong? Do I *still* look like a ghost?

So this year I'm changing my birthday. I've decided that from now on I'll have my birthday on a different day in a different month. This year I will have a happy birthday. Mum won't cry and I'll have a proper birthday cake, not another weird sorbet cake, like the one we had to have for Rory's birthday. Apparently, you can't choke on sorbet and pretending to choke on it is 'not very funny at all'.

If I want to change my birthday the first thing I'll have to do is ask my parents. No, I won't ask them, I'll just tell them.

<u>At breakfast</u>

ME: I'm changing my birthday from the first of March.

DAD: Oh really? Are you going to change your name as well?

ME: Yes. You can call me . . . Supreme Lord Ruler of the World.

DAD: So, Supreme Lord Ruler of the World, when do you want your birthday to be? November?

ME: No. Too close to Christmas.

DAD: August?

ME: Too hot and besides everyone is on holiday in August.

DAD: Everyone? And why does that matter anyway?

ME: Duh! A party is pretty dull if it's just you and a balloon, Dad.

DAD: I see, and it wouldn't have anything to do with the amount of presents, would it?

ME: Erm . . .

DAD: Friendships should be about more than what your

3

friends can give you.

ME: But what about what you said last Saturday night? Mr Henderson brought you a bottle of wine and you said you wouldn't clean the dog's bowl with it.

DAD: I said that?!

ME: Very loudly, or so Greta says. Greta the Great. Thanks for that, what I really needed was to upset the popular girl at school's dad.

DAD: But you didn't say anything! It was me!

ME: Dad, in my world, what you do *is* what I do. If you're mean about someone else's Dad . . . well, I might as well have jumped on the lunch table in a tutu and told the entire school that I still play with Barbie.

DAD: Oh.

So, I'm having my birthday on a different day this year but I just haven't decided when. I'm looking for a sign.

I've already ruled out November, December and August. I can't have it in May because that's my mum's birthday month, June is Grandma's, October is Rory's, January is Grandpa's, February is Aunt Shelly's and my dad's birthday is in September. Which, only leaves April and July. It's the middle of February now, so I've got time to decide, and if I can't decide by the end of March I'll toss a coin instead.

At bedtime

MUM: I hear you're changing your birthday.

ME: Old news.

MUM: Soon you'll be telling me you want a new name too.

ME: No. But I know what I want for my birthday.

MUM: What?

ME: New parents.

2

I've made up my mind. My mum says that when I've made up my mind about something, nothing will ever make me change it again. Sometimes she'll laugh and say, 'You're just like your father. You're as stubborn as a mule.' But I don't mind. I like it when she says I'm like my dad, because even though you are not supposed to have favourites, I think my dad really *is* my favourite.

Anyway, I have made my mind up and my new birthday is going to be on July the fifth. Well, I only had two months to choose from. July the fifth it is.

<u>In the car</u>

DAD: Why the fifth?

6

ME: Er . . . because my name begins with E and E is the fifth letter in the alphabet.

DAD: Oh.

He looked very disappointed and said that it was 'a very unimaginative explanation'.

I didn't want to tell him that the number five was Laura's lucky number.

I didn't want to tell him that sometimes if we were sharing a bag of sweets, Laura would count them out and even if it meant I got more than her, she would always just count out five for herself. Five Skittles, five Maltesers, five Haribos.

Always five.

July the fifth it is. I've circled it on my calendar. Mum doesn't know it yet, but I've changed the date on mine and Laura's birth certificates too. I figured if I was having a new birthday then Laura would want one too.

*

Last night I couldn't sleep. The bed felt lumpy and my eyes just wouldn't stay shut. Maybe it was because Mum didn't come in and say goodnight. She was in *another* mood. 'Dark times' my dad calls it. Well, I wish he'd switch the light on.

I lay there for a long time trying to decide if Greta was right about my haircut. She'd told me at school that even though some of it has grown back, I still look a bit like Shaggy from *Scooby Doo* and I told her that, if we were talking about cartoon characters, she looked a lot like Marge Simpson. I didn't mean to make her cry but everyone said I was being nasty and it wasn't her fault that the swimming pool had turned her hair a funny shade of blue.

I had to spend the rest of the lunch-break sitting on my own, pretending to read a book while Greta and her friends sat by the fire escape staring at me and laughing. The more they laughed and pointed, the more I pretended that the book was the most amazing thing I had ever read – which wouldn't have been so bad had it been the right way up. So I sat there staring at the upside-down pages of my brother's library book and in the end decided that *Rocky Robin and The Rabbits* was much more interesting the wrong way up.

Anyway, I was trying to go to sleep and had just turned on to my stomach when I heard a rustle followed by a very familiar sigh. Then a voice.

VOICE: *July?* Why July?

I lay there completely still. Perhaps it was the telly. Perhaps my mum was talking on the phone. After a while I decided that I had imagined it and I was just drifting off to sleep when I heard a little cough.

VOICE: Er, hello? *Why July?*

I felt my skin prickle and my heart beat a little faster; this time I knew I had not imagined it.

ME: Laura?

VOICE: Yes – Laura, who else would it be?

ME: Is that really you?

The voice went quiet. Perhaps I had been dreaming. Stupid me, I thought. Now I'm hearing voices.

VOICE: Sort of.

I sat up quickly and tried to see around the room.

ME: Well then, what pyjamas am I wearing?

There was a silence and then a sigh.

VOICE: My old ones with the chocolate ice-cream stain on the sleeve.

She was right. We had both been given the same pair of pyjamas for Christmas and one night we had sneaked downstairs, gobbled a whole tub of chocolate ice-cream and hidden the empty tub at the back of the freezer. We would have got away with it if Laura hadn't thrown it all up, all over her bed and the rug in our room. A little bit of chocolate puke had got on the sleeve of her pyjamas too. I rubbed the sleeve with my hand.

VOICE: *Why July?*

ME: Because. I've made my mind up.

My eyes were getting used to the darkened room and I could just make out the side of Laura's bed. I could just see the wardrobe, the globe, the back of my table and chair and the roundish outline of my beanbag.

VOICE: But you didn't ask me. It's my birthday too.
ME: I'm trying to sleep.
VOICE: You've been trying for ages. You could have asked. I'm kind of annoyed to have my birthday changed without even a 'Hey Laura, what do you think to July instead?'

I opened my eyes wider as if that might help me to somehow see in the dark.

ME: I'm going to switch the light on!
VOICE: *Ooh!* Not the snow globe nightlight! I'm really scared.
ME: Well, Laura, as I remember it, it was *you* that was so afraid of the dark that we had to have the nightlight on *all night, every night.*

I didn't mind the dark as long as Mum left the light on in the hall. As long as I could see a little bit of light peeping through the bottom of the door I didn't mind, but Laura always got so funny about it.

One day Grandpa, our dad's dad, came to visit and he brought with him a gift for Laura and I. A little snow globe light. We put it on the third shelf by the door and when Mum or Dad would say goodnight they would switch it on as they left. If they forgot and turned to close the door, Laura would just shout, 'Snow globe!'

Afterwards . . . after *it* happened, I climbed out of my bed one night and unplugged it. Then I made some space on the little table between our beds and plugged it in there instead.

I felt around for the switch and then I heard another rustle.

VOICE: By the way, Greta looks more like Shrek than Marge Simpson.

I laughed, grabbed the switch and turned on the snow globe. The room was empty.

ME: Laura?

Silence.

ME: Laura?

I switched the light off and lay back on the pillow.

ME: Laura . . . I miss you.

I lay there for quite a while, then I switched the globe back on and fell fast asleep.

11

3

The next morning I woke up with a funny feeling. You know, like when you have been dreaming it was the school holidays but you wake up and realise it's just another ordinary *go to school all day and hate it* kind of a day. I walked down the stairs slowly and sat down next to Dad.

DAD: You sleep OK?
ME: I dreamt I was trapped inside a huge snow globe with Shrek and a giant robin.
DAD: That sounds lovely.

He wasn't listening, as usual, then Mum kind of sighed and said, 'James, what's the point in talking to your daughter if you can't be bothered to listen?'

And that was the Breakfast Row started.

I didn't mind that Dad wasn't listening. Laura and I used to see how many things we could say before he noticed.

One morning we got Rory to fill his mouth with Cheerios and then he popped his cheeks so that there was a kind of Cheerio explosion across the table. Dad didn't even put his newspaper down. Laura had smiled at me and said, 'Rory, why don't you do the same with the jam?' So Rory grabbed the little plastic spoon and started gobbling jam from the pot. Laura and I watched in fits of giggles and I think she said, 'He's filling his mouth with jam, Dad. There's going to be jam everywhere, Dad.' But Dad just turned the page of his paper.

Now Mum was doing her horrible screechy voice but at least Dad had put his newspaper down. Their voices got louder and louder and eventually Rascoe, that's our dog, ran back to his basket.

MUM: You have to show an interest, James! There's no point in pretending.

My Dad banged his fist on the table.

DAD: Maybe you should *pretend* to be happy, Fiona!

Pretend to be happy, I thought.

Sometimes I pretend to be happy. Sometimes I pretend to be ill too, and last night I knew that Rory had pretended

13

he'd only had one chocolate biscuit when I knew he'd eaten three.

But Mum didn't want to pretend.

She slammed the kitchen bin lid and then slammed the fridge door shut so hard that Rory's fridge magnet flew across the kitchen and smashed on the floor. Rory burst into tears. I didn't know he liked the magnet so much. Just as well he doesn't know about his monster truck that Rascoe chewed to bits last week.

MUM: Now look what you made me do!
DAD: For goodness' sake! Will you either shut up or go back to bed and leave us *all* alone. We were fine until *you* came down here!

Mum started crying, Rory sobbed a little louder and the dog began to howl.

ME: Laura spoke to me last night.

That shut them up.

Mum stared. Dad stared. So I grabbed my rucksack and left for school.

14

4

I walk to school nearly every day. Some days, when Mum doesn't have to go to work, I walk up the hill with her, Rory and Rascoe.

Rory doesn't go to big school yet, because he's only four, but some days he goes to the little nursery where Laura and I used to go. He seems to love it as much as we did and Mum says that when she drops him off, he makes a run for it and never looks back.

My mum's a maths teacher at the high school. She doesn't go there every day, but one day, when I go there, I really hope (sometimes I even pray) that she isn't *ever* my teacher. I would hate that. Imagine having your mum tell you off in front of everyone? Or imagine if your mum was the teacher that nobody liked?

But this morning I walked up the hill alone.

Again.

I walked past the house with the funny yellow car. It only has three wheels and Dad says it's the stupidest invention ever. He says, 'Can you imagine anything sillier? What were they thinking when they decided that three wheels would be better than four?'

I looked at the car and remembered how Laura used to say that the car looked a bit like a giant piece of cheese because it's kind of triangle-shaped. She used to call it The Cheese Car.

I giggled to myself and waved at the little old lady who was standing at the window of number seventy-three. She's always standing at that window. I wonder if she's stuck to the curtains or something.

In the summer, when it's hot, I hate walking to school because by the time I get there, my face is all red and sweaty.

I don't like it when it's hot and sunny because Mum will always come into my bedroom and say, 'Come on, put that book down and go outside.' But I never know what to *do* when I get outside because we don't really have a garden, just a little square patch of concrete, and Mum says it's too dangerous to go out on the road with my bike. I don't really like playing sports or anything, because I'm not very good at throwing and catching or running and jumping. At least Mum says that I don't have to do sports at school any more. She says that as long as I finish my swimming lessons I don't have to join in with anything else. So now I don't need to be last in every race, throw the ball in the wrong direction or trip over any skipping ropes.

I felt the wind on the tips of my ears so I tried to pull my coat around me, but it's kind of small. The sleeves are way too short and the buttons don't really do up properly. Mum says we have to go and get a new one in the school holidays. I have to have a pair of new school shoes too but Laura and me picked our coats and shoes out together so I don't want any others.

Today it was my favourite kind of weather: icy cold and really sunny. I stopped for a minute to watch a boy I recognised from Mum's school. I think he was the one that got excluded for swearing and throwing a chair at a teacher. It looked like he had one of those scooter things that Mum won't let me have. She says they're dangerous. But she thinks most things are dangerous. That's all Laura's fault. She made birthday cakes dangerous.

I crossed over the road and watched the cars queuing up to get over the huge bridge. It's a special kind of bridge and I can see it from my bedroom window. At night-time the whole thing is lit up with tiny white lights. Dad says people come from all over the world just to walk across it. It's called a suspension bridge because it's sort of suspended really, really high up above the river. It's so high up that if you peek over the edge and look down, it can make you feel sort of dizzy. But I don't really like doing that because I don't really like being high up. My dad is always going on about the man that built it. 'Genius,' he'll say and then he'll try and explain what an 'amazing feat of engineering' it is. But my dad really likes anything to do with bridges. He once drove us all the way to Wales so we could drive across a brand new bridge. When we got home Laura drew a picture of us all driving across it then we stuck it in our special Super-Secret book.

I heard the church bells ring and realised that, despite setting off for school really early, I had somehow managed to become late so I began to run. I ran past the bakery that sells Dad's favourite cakes and past the newspaper shop that sells all the sweets that I love. I ran past Reg the Veg, past the library and through Victoria Square where the stinky man who feeds all the pigeons lives, and then I ran straight into a girl who was running round the next corner. We bumped into each other and I fell backwards onto the pavement.

ME: Ouch! Look where you're going!

She stood up first. The sun was shining right into my eyes and as I squinted up at her, she sighed and put her hands on her hips. I could only make out her silhouette, but even that was pretty scary. Her hair was a mass of wild red curls which seemed to stick out in every direction, making it look like she'd just been struck by lightning.

THE GIRL: Look where YOU'RE going! Two eyes! [She pointed at my face.] For looking in both directions.

I stood up and brushed off the leaves that had become stuck to my jacket.

ME: Don't worry about *me*. I'm not hurt at all.

I put my rucksack back on my shoulders and looked straight into her face. Now I was standing up I could see she was only a little bit taller than me. She was wearing the same St Thomas school uniform as I was, but I had never seen her before. The wind was blowing her hair, but she kept trying to pull it down to cover one side of her face. At first I couldn't see why, because as she spoke she kept turning away from me.

THE GIRL: *You're* the one who wasn't looking! *You're* the one who was looking in the wrong direction!

She was almost shouting at me and that's when I saw what was wrong. She was looking at me with one blue eye, but the other eye was covered with a black eye patch. I gasped.

ME: Wow! A pirate!

I pointed at the patch which she tried to cover up with a strand of curly red hair.

THE GIRL: No, you idiot, and stop staring.

And with that she shoved past me and headed in the direction of my school.

ME: Hey! What's your name? Wait for me!

But she just kept walking, so I ended up running to try and catch up. When I did, she turned around and glared at me.

THE GIRL: Leave me alone!

I followed her in through the gates and into school but by the time I had thought of something less stupid to say than calling her a pirate, she had turned down the next corridor and disappeared.

An eye patch, I thought. That's really cool.

5

After morning register, Miss Cauber told us we would be starting a 'History of Bristol' project, and everyone groaned but me. I like history and maths and English. The only subject I really HATE is art.

I HATE it even more now that Laura isn't here to help me.

Miss Cauber handed out a pile of textbooks and I saw Greta sort of roll her eyes and do a kind of fake yawn. I looked down at the textbook. It really did look dull so I looked back towards Greta and as she turned to face me, I pointed at the book and did the same thing.

MISS CAUBER: Emma! Are you bored already? Sorry, is there something else that you would rather be doing?

The class laughed.

MISS CAUBER: Perhaps you know all there is to know about our great city?

ME: Er . . . no . . . Miss Cauber, I'm sorry but . . .

MISS CAUBER: Perhaps you'd like to teach the class instead?

ME: I was . . . I did . . .

Then I remembered our trip to the library a few weeks ago. Mum had to get some new books for Rory and I had wandered down the aisles until I had come to a section called 'Local History'. I'd had to climb on a little stool to reach the book and Mum said she was very impressed when she saw me reading the grown-up book.

MISS CAUBER: We are all waiting, young lady, stand up please.

I slowly stood up from my chair and felt my cheeks get hot. I felt everyone's eyes on me and my mind raced back to the pages of the book. I closed my eyes and tried to see it. I don't know how it works but if I read something once I can remember it forever – all I have to do is close my eyes and think really hard. Dad says it's called a 'photographic memory' and that I'm lucky to have it. Laura called it my 'magic memory'. It was our secret so I had never shown anyone at school. I tried to see the book.

ME: Bristol is a . . . Bristol is . . .

Everyone sniggered so I closed my eyes again. History of Bristol! History of Bristol! That time it worked. I could see the pages as clear as if the book were right in front of me. I saw the words and the pictures and I opened my eyes with a smile.

ME: Bristol has a rich maritime heritage. By the fourteenth century the city was trading with several countries including Spain, Portugal and Iceland. Ships also left Bristol to found new colonies in the New World. John Cabot set sail in 1497 from Bristol, in his ship *The Matthew*, hoping to find a passage to Eastern Indonesia.

Everyone laughed again but Miss Cauber didn't. Her eyes were really wide and her mouth was sort of gaping open. Then she kind of shook her head. Maybe she wanted something else. I thought for a second and then I remembered another chapter of the book.

ME: Um, The Victoria Rooms is one of Bristol's most impressive buildings. This fine early Victorian classical building was used for readings by Charles Dickens and Oscar Wilde.

I looked up hopefully, but this time Miss Cauber looked a bit like a statue with her hands outstretched in front of her.

I looked around at the class, they weren't really laughing any more but as no one said anything, I took a deep breath and gave it one last try.

ME: In the late eighteenth century, Clifton village grew as merchants relocated and built houses further away from the city docks. By the nineteenth century the success of Bristol's port was beginning to decline. However, the arrival of a new chief engineer, Isambard Kingdom Brunel, helped to attract further investment into the area. Brunel did more than anyone to shape the face of modern Bristol today; his legacy includes the Clifton Suspension Bridge, SS *Great Britain* and Temple Meads railway station . . . Is that enough, Miss Cauber?

Miss Cauber pointed at my seat so I sat down slowly. Everyone was staring and I got the feeling that I shouldn't have said a word.

*

After morning break we had a music lesson. We had to listen to some really old music and then Miss Cauber told us all about the person who wrote it. I wasn't really paying attention until she told us that he had been deaf. I'm not kidding. I had loads of questions, like: how could he write the best music in the world if he couldn't even hear? And what did it feel like to not be able to hear the music that you had written? But Miss Cauber wouldn't let me ask any questions even though I put my hand up for so long it ached. Laura would have laughed and said, 'Serves you right, Smartypants.' She was always calling me that . . .

At break-time I tried to talk to Greta. She was standing by the gates with Erin and Megan.

ME: I . . . err . . . !

I couldn't get the words out, so she just folded her arms across her chest and turned her back to me and then Megan and Erin did the same. I tried again.

ME: Greta, I didn't really mean to . . . err . . .

But she just stuck her fingers in her ears.

GRETA: I can't hear a word you say! Emma Edwards, go away!

I thought about it for a minute and then I remembered what Laura had said.

ME: Laura's right. You do look more like Shrek.

It wasn't the best idea I'd ever had and she burst into tears all over again. So, as usual, I took my book, sat by the sports hut and waited for the bell to ring. It was the second time I had read it and even though I could remember everything about it, break-times weren't too bad if I could disappear into the pages of my favourite book.

After lunch-break, Miss Cauber stood at the front of the class waiting for us to pay attention but everyone was still talking. Eventually she folded her arms across her chest and started tapping her foot. Everyone went quiet – everyone but Josh and Merrick. They were so naughty that last term they got moved to the front of the class. Their desks are right at the front, right under Miss Cauber's stinky coffee breath.

MISS CAUBER: Josh! Merrick! We're all waiting for you.

The two of them sat up and I watched as they hid whatever it was that had been making them laugh underneath the table.

MISS CAUBER: Class Four, today I would like you all to welcome a new pupil. She will be joining us in a minute and I want you all to be as friendly and as welcoming as you can because our new pupil has just moved here from London. Who would like to go to Mrs McWatter's office and show her around the school?

Everyone put their hand up. Everyone but me. Mrs Cauber scanned the class of eager faces and then she put her hand on her hip, sighed and pointed straight at me.

26

ME: But I didn't put my hand up.

MISS CAUBER: Exactly! Now off you go, Emma.

I left the classroom and wandered slowly down the hall. I hated going to see Mrs McWatter because she always wanted me to 'run errands' or to say how 'everyone missed my sister so very much' or ask if I wanted to 'talk'. She didn't seem to understand that it was *me* that missed my sister the most and that talking about it wasn't going to help.

I knocked on the door and waited for what seemed like for ever. Suddenly the door opened and Mrs McWatter let me in.

The sun was shining brightly through the three large windows that looked out on to the playground. It sort of made the room look really hazy and lit up the dust that was floating in the air like magical sparkles. There were book-cases full of books (Mrs McWatter had once told me she had read every one of them) and lots of pictures on the walls of all the school children that had been to St Thomas years and years ago. Among them somewhere was a school picture that was taken in 1980 and on the back row was my mum when she was my age. Then I heard coughing.

MRS MCWATTER: Emma, are you with us?

I looked at Mrs McWatter.

She was wearing something new: a long purple skirt, a silky blouse with pearl buttons, shoes that were kind of shiny and had large purple ribbon bows at the toe. She looked a bit like a birthday present.

Then I turned to the girl who was sitting in the chair opposite Mrs McWatter. It was the girl who I had run into that morning. The girl who was kind of rude. The girl with the red hair and the black eye patch. Suddenly I felt a little scared.

The girl turned to look at me and when she saw it was me who would be giving her the 'grand tour', she stood up and let out a huge 'God! This-is- the-most-boring-day-of-my-life' sigh.

MRS MCWATTER: Emma, I have a very important job for you. [I told you she was always making me run errands]. This is Alexandria Lister.

THE GIRL: Actually, Mrs McWatter, *nobody* calls me Alexandria. I *hate* being called Alexandria and I *hate* being called Alex or Ally or anything like that. Everyone calls me *Lexi*. Just Lexi. Lexi with an I *not* a Y. L-E-X-I. *Lexi*.

Mrs McWatter didn't say anything for a while, she just stood behind her desk, peering over her glasses with her mouth hanging open. I hadn't ever heard anyone speak to Mrs McWatter like that. Then Mrs McWatter took off her glasses and sat back down.

MRS MCWATTER: Err . . . Err, well, I suppose that's fine.

It was really weird. I didn't understand why Mrs McWatter didn't tell Lexi off or shout at her and say something like, 'We do not talk to each other like that at St Thomas School!' Instead she was looking all fidgety and flustery.

I looked at Lexi and held out my hand. She looked down at it, sighed and then she shoved both of her hands inside her jacket pockets. *Fine*, I thought, *I don't want to shake hands with you either! I don't care if you're called Lexi with an I not a Y.*

MRS MCWATTER: Emma, I want you to be especially nice to Lexi because she has just moved here all the way from . . .

She looked down at the bits of paper on her desk. She looked on the floor and pulled open a drawer.

MRS MCWATTER: She has just moved here from, er . . .

She shuffled through the piles of paper, folders and scratched her head. *For a head teacher*, I thought, *she's pretty messy.*

MRS MCWATTER: She's just moved here from . . . Oh, goodness! What have I done with that file?

She bent down and looked underneath a pile of books, underneath the cushion on her seat, underneath the desk. Then I remembered what Miss Cauber had said.

ME: From London?

Lexi giggled.

MRS MCWATTER: What? Oh! Yes! That's right! Well done! From London. So, please give Lexi the St Thomas welcome and take her on a tour of the school. Then you can both go back to class.

Lexi and I left the office and headed down the hallway but I could barely keep up with her because she walked so quickly.

She talked as quickly as she walked. So I didn't hear a word of what she said from outside Mrs McWatter's office all the way to the sports hall where she suddenly stopped, turned around and sniffed. Then she sniffed again.

LEXI: Yuck! Does it always smell like this?

I sniffed a couple of times too.

ME: Like what?
LEXI: Like . . .

She sniffed again then she pinched her nose and pulled a face.

LEXI: Like cabbages.

I laughed out loud. She was right; our school nearly always smells like boiled cabbages.

As we walked out of the hall she was standing to my right so I couldn't see the eye patch. I kept trying to take a peek, so when we walked into the computer suite I moved around to her other side but, as I did so, she pulled some hair across her face. I really wanted to ask why she was wearing it, but every time I opened my mouth to ask her, she started talking again. In fact, she didn't stop talking. She told me where she lived and what her favourite this was and what her favourite that was. She told me that she didn't have any brothers or any sisters. She had moved house four times and she already hated Bristol. But she didn't say anything about the eye patch. Every so often she stopped and fiddled with it a bit and I almost blurted out the question, but my mum says it's rude to ask 'personal questions' of strangers. Laura was always saying things that she wasn't supposed to, like the time we were in the changing rooms at the swimming baths and an old lady was trying really hard to squeeze herself into her jeans and Laura went over to her and said, 'They're a bit too small for you now.'

I waited while Lexi fiddled with her eye patch again and I was just about to show her where the library was when she stopped and turned to face me.

LEXI: Stop it!

ME: Stop what?

LEXI: Stop trying to look!

ME: But . . . but . . . but . . . you're wearing an eye patch! No one wears an eye patch!

31

LEXI: Well, I do, so get used to it.

I didn't know what to say to that.

It was just the sort of thing that Laura would have said and for some reason that made my stomach feel funny.

I didn't say another word until we got back to the classroom. Just before we went inside Lexi turned around and once again she pulled some hair across her face.

LEXI: Thanks. That was the *worst* guided tour I've ever been on.

I didn't say anything.

LEXI: Fine. Stay silent then. I'm used to people being all weird when they see me.

I didn't know what to say to that either so I just turned the handle and pushed open the door. Miss Cauber stood up from her desk and smiled.

MISS CAUBER: Hello! Welcome to Class Four! Come to the front and say hello to everyone.

Lexi didn't move. I didn't move. Everyone turned to look. At first they all smiled. Then I watched as they noticed the eye patch and a whispering began to break out around the classroom. I saw Greta lean over and tap Erin on the shoulder. Even Merrick and Josh stopped mucking about and stared. There was more whispering followed by lots and lots of pointing.

Oh, I thought standing by Lexi's side. *This* doesn't feel very nice at all.

*

At the end of the day I saw Lexi at the school gates. A woman with crazy red hair came running to greet her. She was wearing jeans and a funny-looking top that was covered with paint splatters. She had lots of silver bracelets on her wrists and nearly every single one of her fingers had a ring on it. I looked down at her feet to see if there were bells on her toes, but she was wearing bright red clogs. As she ran towards Lexi, her shoes made a loud *clack, clack* sound and her bracelets made a sort of jangly noise, a bit like a cymbal. I'd never seen anyone like that. I'd never seen anyone who sounded like the entire percussion tray when they moved. She didn't look at all like all the other mums.

CRAZY RED HAIRED WOMAN: Hello, my beautiful girl! How was it?

Then she bent down and kissed Lexi.

LEXI: Hannah! Hannah! Stop it! Get off me, let's go home.

Hannah? So it wasn't her mum, even though they had the same crazy red hair? I saw Lexi push Hannah away and then

33

I watched them climb into a silver car and drive off. Hannah. I knew she was too cool-looking to be a real grown up.

At bedtime

DAD: Goodnight. Oh! How was your day? Anything interesting happen at school?

ME: I met a pirate who went home with a gypsy.

My dad smiled and shook his head. He gave me a kiss on the forehead, then left.

I turned off the snow globe and lay there thinking about Lexi. I wondered why she wore an eye patch and who Hannah really was. I wondered why Lexi had moved house four times.

I've never even moved house once. I was just about to reach for my torch, so that I could read a few more chapters of my book underneath the duvet, when I heard a creaking floorboard. I lay completely still and suddenly I felt quite scared.

VOICE: You know, for someone who is really, really clever you can be so stupid.

ME: Laura?

VOICE: Yes.

ME: I hate school.

There was a long silence then a sigh.

VOICE: How many friends did you *not* make today?

I thought back to the break-time where I had upset Greta and wandered around by myself again.

> ME: I tried to say sorry to Greta.
> VOICE: But you thought you'd tell her she looked like a green ogre instead?
> ME: I only said what you said!
> VOICE: What I said was between you and me and I said it to make you laugh, dummy. You said it to hurt Greta's feelings.
> ME: How am I supposed to know that? How am I supposed to know anything?!

I started to cry, so I turned over and squashed my face into the pillow.

> VOICE: OK, but . . . well . . . sorry . . . don't cry . . . please? At least next time, you'll know. Next time you'll . . .

I pulled the duvet over my head. This was too confusing!

> ME: I don't like any of them. They're all horrid.
> VOICE: All of them?

Then I thought of Lexi. The fastest-talking, fastest-walking, eye-patch-wearing, talks-back-to-Mrs-McWatter-and-gets-away-with-it new girl.

ME: Well, there is someone new.

VOICE: What's her name?

ME: Lexi Lister. She wears an eye patch.

VOICE: Lexi. That's a cool name. And an eye patch, really? Like a pirate?

I laughed out loud. Laura had said exactly the same thing as me. We always thought the same things. We always laughed at the same things. We were the same but we were so different.

I loved reading. She hated it.

I loved numbers and all the maths puzzle books that Mum got for me, but Laura always got her times tables mixed up.

Laura was amazing at painting, but I can't even draw a stick-man properly. She once made a beautiful picture out of broken tiles, but I got the glue everywhere and I even managed to stick my fingers together so we had to go to the hospital to get them unstuck.

Mum always said that I was the 'Science Twin' and Laura was the 'Arty Twin'. So even though we looked *so* alike that people would get us mixed up, we were very, very different. Suddenly, the bedroom door opened and it was Mum.

MUM: It's late. Turn the radio off.

ME: But I don't even have a radio to turn off.

MUM: Oh . . . What was all that noise then?

ME: Nothing.

MUM: Well, goodnight.

She closed the door and I waited until I heard her go down the stairs where she would probably fall asleep in front of the telly.

I pulled the duvet up to my chin. I wondered what Laura would have said if she had been knocked over by Lexi. I wondered what she would have thought of Lexi's wild, curly red hair and her eye patch. Actually, I knew what Laura would have done. She would have asked Lexi straight away and if Lexi wouldn't say why she wore an eye patch, Laura would have just kept on asking and asking until she did.

ME: Laura?

Silence.

ME: Laura?

Silence.

I waited for quite a while but then I felt my eyelids begin to close and the next thing I knew it was the morning.

6

At school it seemed as though everyone had decided that I was weird. I heard Greta call me a name that sounded a bit like, Herd or Merd but I couldn't be sure.

On Wednesday I walked through the library where Greta, Megan and Erin were all sitting together, but when I got closer I could see that Greta was doing a stupid impersonation of me. She had placed an open book on top of her head and she was wearing a really small jacket that looked like it belong to Megan's little sister or something. She walked around the library as though she had two left feet and when she saw me she laughed really loudly and said, 'History of Bristol, blah, blah, blah.' The others started laughing too and as I rushed past them, Greta craned her neck and shouted, ' Freak!'

For some reason Lexi didn't seem to be in the playground much, she was always in the room with the computers and when I asked Miss Cauber why I had to go outside and Lexi didn't, she told me that it was none of my business. Even when Lexi *was* around it seemed like everyone wanted to be friends with her. Everyone was always buzzing around her and it wasn't long before I saw her and Greta together.

On Thursday I was sitting in the classroom reading my book when Miss Cauber found me and told me that I needed to 'get some fresh air'. I didn't want to go outside, and I frowned at her as I watched her put my book on the shelf behind her desk. She turned back to me and pointed to the door.

MISS CAUBER: Out!

I did the biggest sigh I could and went slowly outside. It was so noisy that I wanted to put my hands over my ears. I could hear the boys shouting about their game of football. Everyone was rushing this way and that way.

I walked along the wall and ran my fingers over the bricks. Then I stopped.

For a second I thought I saw her.

I thought I saw Laura!

All the hairs on my body sort of prickled. But when I looked properly it was just a girl from another class. She didn't even really look like Laura . . .

Eventually I went to sit by the sports hut. I sat there

picking at bits of grass and watched the boys play football. I thought about the time that the boys had been fighting over the ball for ages until eventually Laura had just marched over to them, grabbed the ball out of Josh's hands and said, 'I'll decide for you. First one to run to the sports hut. Ready, steady, go!'

She was so bossy, but I didn't mind. And no one else seemed to mind either – not even Greta.

I was just wondering if I could pretend to feel sick or something so I could go back inside when I saw Greta, Megan, Erin and Lexi standing by the fire escape. I could just hear Greta bragging about how her mum works on a television show and how she has met all sorts of really famous people. Greta's always going on about that.

Then I saw Lexi look over to me and Greta whispered something in her ear. I was trying not to listen, but Greta has a very loud high-pitched sort of a voice and every so often I could hear her say the word 'twins' and Laura's name. My stomach did that weird flippy thing again and I don't know why but I really felt as though I was going to cry. I bit down hard on my lip to stop myself and then I remembered Laura's trick. When you want to stop feeling sad, think of the silliest word you can and say it over and over again. The word 'cabbages' popped into my head. *Cabbages! Cabbages! Cabbages! That really is a silly word. Cabbages! Cabbages! Cabbages!* It worked! I did it again but I didn't realise that I was saying it out loud. So loud, that everyone could hear.

40

Greta was the first to start laughing. I watched her shove Erin and Megan and they joined in too. It wasn't long before it seemed to me that everyone was laughing their loudest ever laugh. So I got up and ran, and even though Mr Fincher shouted at me to stay outside, I ran straight into the toilets. I slammed the door shut, locked it and no matter how many times I tried to say the word 'cabbages' I couldn't stop crying. I cried until my head hurt. I cried until the bell rang. I cried until there was a loud knock at the door.

ME: Leave me alone!
LEXI: It's me, Lexi.
ME: Come to laugh at me have you?
LEXI: No, you idiot! Open the door.

I thought about it for a bit. She had just called me an idiot and only Laura got to call me that. I could just see Lexi's shoes under the door, but I stayed still and waited. I saw her tap one foot, but I didn't move.

LEXI: Why are you still crying?

I stopped snivelling.

LEXI: Well?
ME: Why were you all laughing at me?
LEXI: It was kind of hard not to laugh. You did look a bit . . . you know, weird.

41

I huffed and folded my arms across my chest.

ME: Yeah, well not as weird as wearing a pirate costume every day.

Lexi kicked the door so hard the lock sort of rattled, then I saw her feet turn around and she ran out, slamming the door behind her. Why was I so stupid?

I left the toilets and headed back to class, but Mrs McWatter passed me in the corridor, saw my face and said that if I wanted to I could help her tidy up her office. So I spent the rest of the afternoon shuffling bits of paper, shredding envelopes and letters and nearly stapling myself to a rather larger piece of card.

*

When I went to bed that evening, I was so tired that I must have fallen asleep as soon as I turned on my side. I was dreaming of something. I was falling, falling, falling and then *bang*! I just woke up. It sort of gave me a bit of a fright. Not like a nightmare or anything, but like someone had crept up behind me and burst a balloon in my ear.

VOICE: I hate it when that happens.
ME: I thought I saw you today.
VOICE: What else happened today?
ME: Oh, nothing much.
VOICE: Hmm . . . that isn't exactly true, is it?

I thought about lunchtime and Lexi.

ME: I got to miss the afternoon lessons. I helped Mrs McWatter tidy her office.

I rubbed my thumb where I had several paper cuts.

VOICE: You're not very good with a stapler, are you?

I giggled.

ME: At least I didn't have to do drama.
VOICE: Oh I love drama!

It was true. Laura was brilliant at acting out silly things and she was *so good* at doing mime, like pretending she was walking in a snow storm or climbing out of a box or cleaning a window pane. She was amazing at that. I didn't mind drama lessons then. We both went quiet and for a minute I wanted to ask something but I decided not to.

VOICE: And the girl . . . the one with the patch . . . what about her?
ME: She won't like me *now*. I think she's friends with Greta the Great and I HATE Greta.

I heard a little sigh.

VOICE: She's just . . . She's a bit . . .
ME: Horrid and nasty and mean. They were ALL making

43

fun of me, Laura, just because I could remember all that stuff from the book. They were all laughing at me, and she was leading them . . .

I started to cry. What was the use in having a magic memory if no one liked it? What was the use in going to school when no one liked you? If you were on your own all the time?

ME: I don't want to go back . . . I don't want to ever go back there!

I pulled the duvet over my head, curled myself into a ball and cried myself to sleep.

*

The next day I left for school early. I hated walking to school by myself and when I got to the corner where I had bumped into Lexi on her first day, for some reason, I sort of looked out for her. But she wasn't there.

I wandered the rest of the way slowly and occasionally I looked over my shoulder to see if Lexi was behind me.

Her seat was empty when we started class in the morning and she didn't come in at break-time or lunch.

Miss Cauber wouldn't let me have my book back at break-time and she didn't believe me when I said I felt sick and told me to go outside. I could see my book on the shelf behind her desk and for a minute I wondered if I could just grab it when she wasn't looking. But in the end I shuffled outside and sat at the very far corner of the playground with my back to everyone.

*

When I got home from school Rory was upset because Mum had washed his favourite rabbit and it had turned a funny purple-grey colour. He was crying, and crying, as if his rabbit being a different colour was the worst thing that had ever happened. He's so stupid.

So that evening Mum ignored me and spoilt Rory again. He got to stay up really late and eat chocolate-chip biscuits in Mum and Dad's bed.

It was as though I was invisible.

I went into the bathroom to clean my teeth. I looked at myself in the mirror. I looked at my boring brown hair which was still a bit sticky-uppy and wished I had crazy red hair. I went into my bedroom and looked over at the two beds. Above the bed by the window, in big silver letters, was the name Laura and above my bed, in big gold letters, was my name. *I hate my name*, I thought. So, I went over to Laura's bed, pulled back the duvet and climbed inside.

I lay there and waited.

I waited until I heard my dad come home and then I waited for him to come and say goodnight. But he didn't.

I waited for my mum to come and kiss me goodnight. But she didn't.

I waited and waited for Laura to speak to me. But Laura didn't come that night either. And I felt sadder and lonelier than I had ever felt in my whole entire life.

45

7

Today is February the twenty-eighth and normally I would be getting really excited.

Normally I would have been looking forward to getting birthday presents. Laura and I would have made a list of all the things we wanted. But this year I didn't make a list. I didn't want to make a list without Laura.

My dad used to say, 'You two are a whole bundle of wants.' I always wanted a new book (it's not my fault that I can read so fast) and Laura always wanted some kind of stickery glittery thingy. But this year my birthday was going to be on July the fifth and even though July the fifth was a long way off, I just couldn't think of anything I really, really wanted.

At breakfast

DAD: Are you really sure you want to have a new birthday?

ME: I want a new everything.

DAD: *Everything?*

ME: New birthday, new name, new hair, new mum, new . . .

I burst into tears. But the scariest thing was when I looked up again my dad was crying too. I had never, *ever* seen my dad cry. Not once.

DAD: Your hair is lovely, your name is the prettiest name in the world – I should know, I choose it for you – and your mum . . . well, your mum is . . .

I held Dad really tightly and snuggled my face into his side. I love my dad's cuddles, they are the best cuddles in the world especially as Mum seems to have forgotten how to. Dad looked down at my face and with a tissue he wiped the tears away from my cheeks.

DAD: I'm sorry. I'm so sorry you're feeling sad.

I don't know why he was saying sorry, it wasn't *his* fault. Dad never did anything wrong, but my mum always seemed to be cross at him for something. She was cross with him for being at work so much, she was cross at him for not emptying the kitchen bin and last month she was *really* cross at him for

47

leaving his mug on the side of the bath – so cross that she threw the mug across the room and it smashed against the kitchen wall. Dad hadn't said anything. He just told me to take Rory upstairs and I could hear them arguing about it for ages. Mum kept saying things about Laura and Dad kept saying things about money and in the end Rory and I sang 'The Wheels on the Bus' until they stopped.

Dad looked down at me and smiled. His face was all prickly and there were lots of toast crumbs around his mouth.

DAD: So, as tomorrow is your average, everyday, run-of-the-mill, boring old Sunday, you wouldn't want to go to the cinema, have a MacDonald's and go and see Grandma afterwards, would you?

I jumped down from my seat.

ME: Oh, yes I would! Yes I would! But no Rory, please? Just you and me!
DAD: You don't have anyone else you'd like to invite?

Anyone else, I thought. I didn't have anyone I'd like to invite to a 'it's not really my birthday any more' treat. Then I realised I wouldn't have anyone to invite to my new birthday in July either, which made my tummy go funny again.

ME: Just us, please.
DAD: OK. Just the two of us.

Dad and I had the best day ever, even though it was just a boring old 'it's not really my birthday any more' day.

In the morning we took Rascoe for a walk, which meant we had to go across the bridge to the park on the other side. Rascoe immediately made friends with another dog who was almost twice as big as him and the two of them went running off into the woods together. *Huh*, I thought, *even my dog can make friends more easily than me.*

Then we went to see a film and Dad bought the most enormous tub of popcorn that I have ever seen, but as we were going inside I saw Greta and Lexi queuing up for sweets. I tried really hard to make myself invisible so they didn't see me.

After the film we walked across the car park and even though I was full up from all the popcorn, I ate a McDonald's as well because we're only allowed to eat it a few times a year. Mum says, 'That food is no good for anyone. It's full of junk,' but I always say, 'Duh, Mum! It's called junk food! It's supposed to be full of junk.'

Dad and I sat down by the window and I took a slurp from my strawberry milkshake. When I looked up again my dad had stuck two straws up his nose and one in each ear. I burst out laughing, but then I saw Greta and Lexi sitting at the table opposite, so I stopped. They were both sort of staring and suddenly I didn't feel like eating the rest of my food. I didn't even feel like an ice-cream and I can always make room for one of those no matter how stuffed I am.

<u>In the car on the way to Grandma's house</u>

DAD: What's up, Chicken?

I said nothing and carried on staring out of the window.

DAD: Chicken?

ME: Stop calling me that! Do I cluck?

DAD: No.

ME: Do I have lots of feathers?

DAD: No.

ME: Am I terrified of foxes and do I taste delicious with mashed potatoes?

DAD: OK! OK, *Miss Edwards*. What's up with you?

Dad turned off the radio and at first I thought he was going to tell me off but *I* was cross with him and his silly straws.

ME: Did you have to do that with the straws? Did you have to embarrass me?

DAD: But you found it funny, didn't you?

ME: Well, yes, but . . .

DAD: That's all that matters then, isn't it?

I didn't really know what to say to that. He was right, it *was* funny. One time when we had all been out together my mum had done the silly straw thing too. Only she put two straws in her mouth so that she had two straw fangs. I giggled to myself as I remembered how Laura had laughed so much that she had spat a bit of her strawberry milkshake over the table.

Dad was right. It was funny and I didn't care what anyone thought. *I didn't care at all.*

That night I had to read Rory a bedtime story because Mum had gone to bed with another headache. After I said goodnight to Dad who was reading his book in the bath, I crawled into Laura's bed again. I was just about to fall asleep when I had a feeling that I wasn't alone.

VOICE: That's my bed.

ME: And?

VOICE: It's the second time you've slept in my bed. What's wrong with yours?

ME: Your duvet is softer and . . . anyway why does it matter to you? It's not like you need it any more.

VOICE: How do you know that?

I sat up suddenly, and even though the lights were off, I could just about see around the room. I thought I saw a shadow or something. I switched the light on. But there was nothing there . . . No shape. No shadow. No ghostly anything. I turned the light off and lay back on the bed, but after a while I changed my mind, got up and climbed back into my own bed.

VOICE: That's better. Oh, and even though it's not our birthday any more, happy birthday us.

ME: Happy birthday us.

VOICE: Night.

ME: Night, Laura.

That night I dreamt that Laura and I were fighting the evil MacDonald's Straw Monster. But in my dream I was wearing an eye patch and Laura didn't have straight brown hair, she had bright red, wild, curly hair.

8

On Monday everything was back to normal. Lexi came to school late and Erin and Greta were busy swapping their special sparkly keyrings again. When Miss Cauber came in to take the register, I tried to smile at Lexi, but she wasn't looking my way, then Miss Cauber tapped her pencil on her table.

MISS CAUBER: Everyone listen! Yesterday was a very special day for somebody, wasn't it?

Miss Cauber looked over at me and my cheeks went bright red.

MISS CAUBER: Shall we all sing a belated 'Happy Birthday'?

This is what we do at St Thomas. If it's your birthday, you go to the front of the class, everyone stands up and then they all sing 'Happy Birthday', really loudly. Miss Cauber smiled and pointed at me.

MISS CAUBER: Come along, Emma.

I didn't move a muscle. It wasn't my birthday yesterday. I had a *new* birthday. My birthday was July the fifth. Why hadn't my mum said anything to Miss Cauber? Now everyone was looking at me and I felt my heart beat quickly like it does when I get very nervous. But I wasn't really nervous. I was really cross. I didn't want everyone to sing me the silly birthday song now.

MISS CAUBER: Yesterday's birthday girl, come here!

But before I had a chance to say anything, everyone stood up and started singing 'Happy Birthday' and for some reason, this time it seemed as though they were singing it especially loudly. Miss Cauber was clapping and even Josh, who has the worst singing voice in the world, was singing along. I felt myself get angrier and angrier until I opened my mouth and in the loudest voice I have ever used I shouted:

STOP IT! STOP IT! STOP IT! STOP SINGING THAT STUPID SONG! IT WASN'T MY BIRTHDAY YESTERDAY! IT'LL NEVER BE MY BIRTHDAY ON

MARCH THE FIRST EVER, EVER, EVER AGAIN! I HAVE A NEW BIRTHDAY! I HAVE A BRAND NEW BIRTHDAY! JULY THE FIFTH! JULY THE FIFTH! JULY THE FIFTH!

My whole body was shaking and by the time I had finished shouting, everyone had sat back down.

Miss Cauber had dropped her pencil and was staring at me with her mouth wide open. Even Mr Fincher, who was teaching across the hall, had come to see what was going on.

I looked around at all the faces that were staring at me. Everybody looked as though someone had blown a giant trumpet right into their face. They looked really frightened and it was so quiet that I could only hear the panting of my own breath and the hammering of my heartbeat.

Then I heard the sound of a loud sigh and when I looked over to the back of the classroom I saw Lexi. She folded her arms across her chest and tipped her head to one side.

LEXI: July the fifth?
ME: Yes! July the fifth!
LEXI: That's my birthday too.

And for some reason that made both of us burst out laughing.

*

After the 'shouting incident', Miss Cauber told me that the next time I wanted to change my birthday, all I had to do was

55

tell her nicely. Actually, she made me stay behind at break-time and help her with a display she was arranging in the art corner.

It was the project we had done before Christmas. A teacher from my mum's school had come in every Monday for a whole month. She talked to us about pottery and sculpture and that sort of thing. Then we had to design and make something. 'Something' being the right word for my creation. I had definitely made 'something'.

It wasn't quite a dish or a cup. It wasn't quite a plate or a jug. It wasn't painted or decorated like all the other girls had done. It was a 'something' but no one could really work out what the 'something' was. Miss Cauber said it was 'interesting', but I just thought about how Laura would have laughed if she'd seen it. She would have laughed and laughed and I was thinking about smashing the stupid 'something' accidentally on purpose when Miss Cauber took it out of my hands.

MISS CAUBER: We don't shout at each other like that at St Thomas School, do we?

I stared past her shoulder and out of the window where Josh and Merrick were fighting over who got to be in goal.

ME: Josh and Merrick always shout. They're always shouting at each other. They're always screaming [and I did my best Merrick impersonation], 'Give me the ball, give me the ball. Give me the ball, you idiot, you'll never score from there. PASS ME THE BALL!'

Miss Cauber sighed, shook her head at me and said that maybe I needed some quiet time in the computer suite. She said that if I wanted to I could take my book with me. So I did.

So now I know. When I don't want to go outside at break, next time I want to just stay inside with my book, all I have to do is shout really, really loudly.

I wandered into the computer room slowly and sat down on the blue chair by the window.

I don't know why I didn't see her at first, perhaps I was looking at the floor or something, because sitting at a computer, in the far corner by the large bookcases, was Lexi. By the time she turned to face me I was already staring. We looked at each other for what seemed like for ever. I think she was sort of smiling. I think we were both waiting for the other to say something first. I watched as she twirled one of her red curls round and round her finger and for some stupid idiotic reason I decided to say what my mum used to say to Laura if she saw her twirling her hair. Before I had a chance to think, I said in a very school teacher sort of a way, 'It'll get all tangled up if you do that.'

Lexi just sighed, shook her head and turned away from me. I felt my cheeks go all hot. Even though I had a weird magic memory, even though I could add up sums like a human calculator, I was in fact A BIG FAT MORON.

Mum came to meet me after school that day and she made me and Rory wait in the library so she could have a 'little chat' with Miss Cauber. I tried to keep Rory entertained, but Rory doesn't really like to sit still for very long. He just wants to hide in the smallest places he can find. So while Mum and my teacher were probably talking about how I had screamed at the whole class like a crazy person and frightened everyone, I had to try and free my little brother from inside the paper bin.

On the way home Mum didn't tell me off or anything so when we got to the door of Kaycees, I asked if we were allowed to buy some sweets.

Rory's eyes lit up and he ran inside the shop shouting, 'Weeties! Weeties for Rory!' In the end Mum had to go and get him out of the shop because he stuffed a handful of fizzy cola bottles into his mouth and quickly became attached to a *Thomas the Tank Engine* comic. When she tried to pull the comic out of his tiny hands, he let out a scream that made my ears ring. It was what we all call the 'Rory Roar'.

MUM: Roreeeee! Stop that NOW!
RORY: I want Thomas! I want Thomas!

Mum picked Rory up but he started screaming even more. He beat his little fists against her chest and kicked his legs so hard that one of his red wellies flew across the shop and hit the woman at the counter on the head.

58

I tried not to laugh, but it was hard because the more Mum tried to stop him, the worse Rory got. He kicked, he punched and then he pulled some of her hair. It looked as though Mum was wrestling with an octopus, but then she sort of dropped him and the roaring octopus started screeching. That was the moment when Lexi walked in.

LEXI: Wow. That's super-loud, for someone so small.

When Lexi saw me she kind of stopped smiling and turned away. I was just about to explain how nothing got in between my brother and 'Tommy Tank Engine' when Lexi turned back towards me and I *looked straight at her patch*. For a second we both just stood still facing each other until Rory ran over and pointed straight at Lexi's patch. She turned to one side and pulled a strand of hair across her face and Rory ran over to Mum.

LEXI: Is that your brother then?

I said nothing and stared at her handful of strawberry laces.

LEXI: Oh, this is the bit where you go all funny on me, isn't it?

Even though my brain was screaming at me to talk, I didn't know what to say. I was scared I would say something stupid like, 'Sweets aren't very good for your teeth, you know.' I bit my lip and held my breath. Lexi just shook her head.

LEXI: Whatever!

So, before I had a chance to pretend that Rory wasn't my brother or in any way related to me, before I had a chance to get my brain to work properly so that I could actually say something normal, she did a sort of loud 'tut' sound, paid for her strawberry laces, turned around and left the shop.

Eventually Mum and me calmed Rory down with some chocolate stars, but when we left the shop I saw Lexi and Greta sitting on the bench outside. As I walked past I heard Greta say, 'Yeah and I'm changing my birthday too. No, actually I'll have three birthdays this year!' I could hear her laughing all the way down the street.

*

Mum didn't say much to me after we got back, she was too busy 'dealing with Rory' who was making the most of all the attention he was getting.

All she made me for dinner was a toasted sandwich which she left on the kitchen table. I spent for ever picking out the bits of tomato. Mum had forgotten that it was Laura who liked tomato, not me. Rascoe looked up at me hopefully but even he didn't fancy warm, squishy tomato.

I ate on my own and then watched a bit of telly and when Mum started moaning about all the washing that 'I had made for her' I went upstairs to bed.

I finished my book and as I went to put it back on the shelf, I noticed that a photograph frame that was on the top of the bookshelf had fallen on its face. I turned it over. It was a photo of me and Laura. It was the one Grandpa had taken of us at the hot air balloon festival.

Every year hundreds of people come to Bristol from all over the world with lots of special hot air balloons, and one year Grandpa had come to spend the whole weekend with us so he could see them too. In the morning we all walked up the hill together. We had got up really early so that we could watch them fly over the bridge. There were lots of hot air balloons – some were shaped like animals, some like the planets and some were made up of every single colour in the rainbow, but my favourite one was shaped like a car.

Mum had brought a breakfast picnic and we all sat on the grassy hill behind the bridge and when Laura and I waved up at one of the brightly coloured balloons, the person inside had hung right out of their basket and shouted, 'Good morning, Bristol.' It was amazing! Laura said that when she was big enough she would fly over the bridge in her very own hot air balloon. But I said I wouldn't ever want to do that because I don't really like to be too high up, I get sort of dizzy. Grandma once said that me and Laura were so hard to tell apart, that it was just as well I was the twin with my feet on the ground and Laura was the twin with her head in the clouds.

I climbed into bed and switched off the snow globe. I

turned on my side and looked over at Laura's bed. Sometimes I hated seeing it all flat and empty. I squeezed my eyes shut and waited.

ME: Laura? Are you there?

Silence.

ME: Laura, please talk to me.

I waited and waited but there was nothing, just the faint sound of the TV from downstairs. I turned over, squashed my face into my pillow and tried not to cry, but then I heard the door open. I turned around and as I could just see the top of a tiny head I knew *exactly* who it was.

ME: Rory! Go back to bed.

But the next thing I knew his little face was about an inch from my nose, so I switched on the snow globe. He was wearing a pair of my old pyjamas and tucked under his arm was Laura's little rabbit.

ME: Where's your rabbit?
RORY: It's all wurple.

I remembered the washing machine drama. I remembered how Mum had spoilt Rory and ignored me as usual.

ME: Go back to bed, Squirt! And you mean *purple*, Rory. It's not wurple, it's *purple*. Say p, p, p, purple.

Rory blinked up at me.

RORY: P, p, p, p . . . wurple.

I laughed and looked down at my little brother. His pyjama bottoms were too big for him, Mum had rolled them up at the bottom and at the waist, but he still looked like he was drowning in pyjamas. He was kind of cute. Why couldn't he have been 'cute little Rory' in the sweet shop? Why did he have to be 'Monster Rory', 'Horrid Rory', 'Scream until I get what I want Rory'? Why did he have to be like that when Lexi walked in? Why did he have to point at her face?

ME: Rory, go back to bed!

I put my face back in my pillow. Then I heard a little snivel and the bedroom door opened and closed behind him.

VOICE: You idiot! You should have given him a cuddle.
ME: Firstly, you're kind of bossy for someone who isn't really here. Secondly, you were the one who choked on a bit of cake so I think you'll find it's you who's the idiot. Plus why do you only seem to turn up when you want to tell me off?

Then I heard Mum talking to Rascoe which meant she was on her way upstairs. I decided that as I was already in her bad books I didn't want to upset her more by arguing with my dead sister. That would definitely make her mad.

9

Now that everyone in my class knew I had a very loud, shouty, scary voice, I thought things would change somehow, but it seemed to me that absolutely everything was EXACTLY THE SAME. Except On Tuesday lunchtime, when I was queuing up for my food, Josh walked by and said, 'I'm starving'. It was two more words than he had *ever* said to me before and it was quite nice that someone was actually speaking to me for a change, but then I watched him wipe a bogey on the back of Merrick's jumper and then Merrick grabbed something out of the bin and wiped it down Josh's trousers. Mr Fincher shouted at both of them to go and sit outside Mrs McWatter's office. *Huh*, I thought, *being happy that one of those snotty, fart-bags has spoken to me means only one thing*: THAT I AM A TOTAL LOSER.

I looked around the lunch hall for an empty seat and ended up having to sit down by a group of girls in the year below me and as I munched on my macaroni cheese, I watched Greta leave the lunch hall with Lexi. Greta leant towards Lexi and whispered something into her ear and at the very last minute Lexi turned and looked at me. When she saw I was watching her, she sort of glared at me. Even though I had chosen a new birthday which just happened to be on the same day has her *actual* birthday, it seemed that she was one of *them* and preferred to be friends with someone less shouty, scary and weird than me.

*

That night, when I was lying in bed, I heard Mum and Dad arguing again. Dad had got home late from work and Mum was telling him off for being 'selfish' and 'incon-something or other'. Then she said, 'My work is just as important as yours!'

That was the moment when my dad started shouting at my mum too, which woke Rory up and he started crying.

Mum came running up the stairs, so I quickly switched off the snow globe. She'd already been up twice to tell me to go to sleep and she'd taken my book off me, but I'd just climbed out of bed and grabbed another one off the shelf.

I hid it under the covers and waited for her to go back downstairs.

I could hear her fussing over Rory.

MUM: 'It's OK Rory, it wasn't, Mummy and Daddy shouting. It was just the telly.'

66

So now Mum is pretending to be happy. I have to pretend not to be sad and my little brother has to pretend that my parents aren't really shouting at each other.

I lay there for a while, listening, and then I felt myself falling asleep when I heard a creaking sound.

VOICE: Macaroni cheese again for dinner?

It was my one of my favourites but Laura had hated it. She said it looked like dog sick.

ME: Do you still hate it?
VOICE: I'll always hate it.
ME: For ever?
VOICE: For ever and ever.
ME: Do you think Mum and Dad will stop having fights?
VOICE: I hope so.
ME: Me too. They didn't always argue, did they?
VOICE: The only time I ever heard Mum shout was that time I tipped a whole carton of milk into her work bag one morning because you didn't want her to go back to work.

I'd forgotten all about it.

ME: Yeah and her bag kind of smelt really bad afterwards.

We both laughed.

VOICE: Oh, remember they had a sort of row when Dad got us all really badly lost on the way back from holiday and he wouldn't ask anyone for directions?

ME: And we almost ran out of petrol.

It was on the way back from our first camping trip and Dad thought it would be a really good idea to visit Grandpa in his new cottage. We hadn't been there before so Laura and I were really excited about seeing the little stone cottage on the sandy beach. We couldn't wait to see Grandpa, but Dad took a wrong turning somewhere and we ended up driving for hours down a really windy road. It was so twisty and turny that Mum and Laura both got badly car sick and . . .

VOICE: You know, you're not a total loser.

I smiled.

VOICE: It's just that you do a really good impression of one.

We both sort of laughed and that night I fell asleep quickly without crying or anything like that.

*

The next morning I came down the stairs and saw the new shoes that were waiting for me. I didn't like them. I didn't want them. Mum had told me I needed new shoes and it looked like she had just bought them without me. She'd said that I couldn't go on squeezing my feet into my old shoes. She told me that she'd seen a pair that were perfect and that I would really like them. But I didn't. I hated them. They had laces for a start and Laura hated laces. I picked up the box and shoved them in the cupboard under the stairs where they would stay with all the other unloved and unwanted things.

<u>At breakfast</u>

ME: Where are Mum and Rory?

Dad looked up from his newspaper.

DAD: Mum's taken him into nursery.
ME: But we were supposed to go to school together. I don't want to walk on my own again.

Dad put down his toast.

DAD: Why don't *we* walk up the hill together instead?

Dad *never* walked me to school. He was *always* too busy and in too much of a rush. He always had to go into university and do experiments. He always had something more important to do. I looked over at Rascoe.

ME: Can we take Rascoe?

Dad shook his head.

DAD: I can't take Rascoe to work.

Rascoe looked miserable but Dad was right, you couldn't take a dog into a science laboratory.

ME: Will you be exploding things today?

He laughed. I once heard my mum call him an 'overgrown student', but really he's a scientist. In fact, he's something called a volcanologist, which is someone who knows all about rocks and earth and things. Once he even brought a tiny bit of moon rock home to show me and Laura (but don't tell anyone because he wasn't supposed to).

Dad shoved the last piece of toast into his mouth and sighed.

DAD: No. Not today. Just boring lab work.
ME: You do realise that I have no idea what that means, don't you?
DAD: Well, today I will be looking at lots of teeny-weeny bits of rock and then I will do lots of tests on every single little bit.

He went over to the cupboard, took out a jar, popped a 'fit and strong tablet' in my hand and passed me a glass of juice.

DAD: Down the hatch, eh?

I giggled. He always says that. Actually, Dad always says the exact same things at the exact same time. Like, if he farts he always laughs and says, 'Better out than in, eh?' Or if he eats up my or Rory's leftovers, he'll wink and say, 'Waste not, want not.' Laura used to call him the 'human dustbin', but Mum says he's just really greedy.

We set off a bit late and chatted about nothing in particular. Then just as we reached the house with the funny little yellow car, Dad looked at me.

DAD: What did you mean the other day when you said you had spoken to Laura?

I felt my cheeks go red and for a millisecond, for a nanosecond, I almost told him why. Then I looked up at the yellow car.

ME: Look! It's the cheese car.

Dad laughed.

DAD: Stupidest invention in the world.

Then he turned to me, sort of frowned and rubbed his chin.

DAD: I was thinking about what you said and I wondered . . .

But then I saw that the little old lady was standing by the window again.

ME: I wonder why she's always standing at the window?

Dad turned around, craned his neck and at that moment a little van stopped in front of the house. He pointed as a man with a pile of envelopes and parcels climbed out of the driver's side.

DAD: She's just waiting for the postman.

Oh, I thought, *that's a really dull explanation*. That's not as interesting as being stuck to the curtains. But at least I had stopped my dad asking any more questions about my bedtime chats with Laura. And even if I did tell him or anyone else, they wouldn't believe me. You wouldn't, would you?

As we were walking towards the school gates, I spied Lexi getting out of a car. I tugged at my dad's sleeve, he bent down towards me and I whispered into his ear.

ME: Dad, that's the new girl.

Dad looked over my head.

ME: I thought we could be friends. She's a bit like . . .

I stopped for second. She *was* like someone. Maybe.

ME: And even though we have the same birthday, I don't think she likes me but now she's friends with Greta and the others anyway. Greta is just a big old mean-bag – she's always pointing and talking about me.

Dad sighed and turned to face me.

DAD: Aren't you doing exactly the same thing right now?

I looked over at Lexi as she put her rucksack on and fiddled with her patch again. I looked over and realised I *was* still pointing.

ME: And she's really secretive about why she wears an eye patch.
DAD: Look, if she wants to tell you why she's wearing it, she will. But maybe . . . maybe you should just treat her like you would if she wasn't wearing it? You know, would you like it if everyone treated you differently because of Laura?

I thought about it for a second and wondered how he could be so stupid. Then I turned to him and in my new super-shouty, very loud and scary voice I said:

ME: BUT EVERYONE DOES TREAT ME DIFFER-ENTLY BECAUSE OF LAURA, YOU IDIOT!

Dad looked at me as though I had stamped on both of his feet so I just turned around and ran into school.

*

When I got to class, Miss Cauber said that as it was the last day of term everyone could have half an hour of 'Free Choice' time, which meant we could pick anything to do, well nearly anything.

Josh and Merrick ran outside with a few other boys and played football and Greta asked if she could help Miss Cauber with any jobs.

I did what I always do: I took my book and went to find the quietest spot I could. I went to the library but there was a bunch of other kids in there so in the end I sat in the corner of the computer suite.

I was just getting comfy when Lexi came in. I looked up from my book and watched her touch her patch as she walked across the room. I tried to ignore her but she sat down at the computer next to me. I tried not to look at her but it felt as though something was pulling my head up. It felt as though no matter how hard I tried to keep on reading, something was stopping me from looking down at the pages. Suddenly Lexi turned and looked at me.

LEXI: You're reading AGAIN. How boring!

She turned back to the computer screen.

ME: You don't have to be mean, you know.

74

I waited. My eyes stayed glued to the side of her head until she turned to face me.

LEXI: And you don't have to stare.

I gulped, looked down at my book and tried to ignore her, but I wanted to know what she was doing. I craned my neck a little and saw that she was on the internet. I don't really like computers but Lexi *always* seemed to choose to use the computers if we had 'Free Choice' time. After a while there was a loud clacking sound as Lexi started typing and I decided that I would have to find somewhere else to read but as I walked behind her, I quickly glanced at the screen.

To:EthanC@hotmail.com
From Lexiland@hotmail.com
Hi Ethan! That was really funny. Did your mum see that?

She turned around and glared at me.

LEXI: Hey! Get lost!

Lexiland? Where was that? And who was Ethan? Lexi put her hands over the screen.

LEXI: Go away, you freak!

I was just about to say something back when I remembered what my dad had said and I realised that Lexi was right. I *had* been staring at her. I always seemed to do stupid things when she was around. It was like she made me a bit nervous or something. No wonder she didn't like me and as I was the one who talked to my dead sister – I *must* be a freak.

10

Saturday morning was the first day of the Easter holidays and I was feeling really pleased that at least I had two whole weeks where I could have lie-ins, read until my head hurt and, if I was lucky, Dad might even take me to cinema again.

After breakfast I went back to my room and climbed on to the bedside cabinet so that I could reach my hiding place. I felt around on the top of the wardrobe until my fingers reached what I was looking for.

Our special Super-Secret book had got all dusty as it had been such a long time since I last got it out. I hadn't looked at it since Laura had . . .

I sat down on my bean bag and looked inside. On the first page was a picture that Laura had drawn of the two of us and underneath it she had decorated our names with sequins and pink and purple feathers. On the next page was her painting of the bridge and underneath that was the story that I had made up. It was a really silly story, but Laura had loved reading my silly stories and I had loved looking at her pictures.

Laura hated having to do any school reading. She used to throw a total wobbly if Mum made her read because she thought all the school book stories were boring and stupid, but she always wanted to read mine. Whenever she was poorly or feeling sad, I would make up a new story just for her, and she especially liked it when I did different voices.

I turned the pages of the book until I finally found the picture I was looking for. It was a pencil drawing of a hot air balloon. Laura had coloured the balloon in with every single colouring pencil that she had. I was in the picture too, but I was standing underneath on the side of the bridge and Laura was in the basket looking down, me with my feet on the ground and Laura with her head in the clouds. Laura had drawn her hair so it looked as though the wind was blowing it around and Mum and Dad were standing on either side of her. She was smiling her big Laura smile and by the side of the basket she had drawn a speech bubble and in her lovely handwriting she had written, 'Up, up and away!'

I was just about to read the story that went with the picture when I heard a knock at the door. I hid the book underneath the bean bag and Dad came in and sat down on Laura's bed.

DAD: So, what are you doing?
ME: Nothing.
DAD: What you gonna do tomorrow?
ME: Nothing much.
DAD: Well, instead of 'nothing' and 'nothing much' would you like to have an adventure?

I quickly tried to think of all the adventurous things that we could do but my mind went kind of blank.

DAD: Mum is taking Rory to London to see Aunt Shelly for a few days, so she's taking Rascoe up to stay with Grandma and we're going to Grandpa's house.

Rory was going to Aunt Shelly's? She's my mum's little sister and she's *really* cool and funny. Aunt Shelly is nothing like Mum at all. Mum is tall and Shelly is kind of titchy. Mum has straight brown hair, like me, and Shelly has really long blonde hair (Laura and I used to say that she looked like Rapunzel) and if she gives you a kiss you always get a big red lipstick kiss mark on your cheek. Once Mum told me and Laura to go and get a tissue and wipe it off but we had both left it on until bedtime. I always had the bestest time when we went to visit her in her teeny weeny flat. I loved it there. And whenever Mum went to see Aunt Shelly she always seemed happy.

ME: Why isn't Mum taking me too?! Why does Rory get to go? Why does the little piglet get to go with Mum?

I was just about to start crying when Dad bent down, put his finger under my chin and lifted my face up to his.

DAD: Rory isn't a little piglet.
ME: He roars like a lion and he snores like a piglet!

Dad laughed.

DAD: OK, so your little brother does kind of snore like a piglet, but a very sweet little piglet. Look, your mum and I thought it would be a good idea for us all to have a break from one another for a while, and *I* want to spend time with you. *Just you.* No piglet snoring and no Rory Roar. Besides, you haven't seen Grandpa for a very long time. It'll be fun. It'll be an *adventure*.

I know lots of things about my Grandpa, but none of them were as interesting as Aunt Shelly and her princess hair. He moved house a lot and he travelled all over the world writing about places to go on holiday and stuff like that. He was brilliant at taking photographs too because nearly all of the pictures in our house were taken by him.

ME: Where does Grandpa live now?

My dad stood up and closed the window.

DAD: Well, do you remember the cottage on the beach?
ME: Of course, me and Laura were just saying that . . .

I stopped suddenly and looked down.

ME: I mean, me and Laura went there loads.

Dad looked down at me funny.

DAD: Well, do you remember me telling you that he was
moving back to Oxford?

I nodded. Oxford was where my dad had grown up. Dad
turned around and straightened the E in the gold letters
above my bed.

DAD: Grandpa lives in a houseboat now . . . well, it's a
sort of houseboat.

A *houseboat!* I'd never seen one of those. I'd never even heard
of one before.

ME: Dad, what is a sort of houseboat?
DAD: You'll see when we get there because you and I
are going to give Grandpa a house-warming present.
Well, a houseboat-warming present. We're going to

Oxford! Now grab a few things, we're leaving in an hour.

Mum helped me to pack a bag. We couldn't find my going-away rucksack, so I used my school bag instead. I put in a new book, the Super-Secret book and Laura's little rabbit. When I hugged Mum goodbye, she squeezed me tightly for what seemed like for ever and when I looked up at her face it looked like she was about to cry but she suddenly smiled at me and stroked the top of my head.

ME: What's the matter, Mum?

She smiled and buttoned up my coat.

MUM: Oh, nothing, never mind. Have fun.

In the car Dad played his favourite music and we both sang along all the way to the service station. Although my dad can't really sing properly and neither can I. I didn't mind, I was getting really excited.

A *houseboat*, I thought, *this really could be an adventure after all*. I tried to imagine what the houseboat would look like. I imagined a sort of sailing ship with our house sitting on top. Then I imagined a huge ferry boat with a mansion or a massive ocean cruise ship with a block of flats sitting on top.

Only then I did what I always do on long motorway journeys: I fell fast asleep. I dreamt that I was living on a pirate ship and instead of sails, it was being pulled along by three giant hot air balloons.

When I opened my eyes again we were already in Oxford and Dad had stopped the car in a large car park.

I looked around for signs of ships and ferry boats, but there was nothing. We got out of the car and crossed over to the other side and that was when I saw the water. But it wasn't the sea or anything. It wasn't a wild river. It wasn't anything exciting.

DAD: This [He pointed down at the murky water] is the canal.

We walked down some steps to a sort of narrow pavement.

DAD: And this is a special kind of path. Look, it's on both sides of the water. It's called the tow path.

I looked down at the tow path but it just looked like a pavement to me.

DAD: Years ago people used these canals like motorways, like railways. Remember when I told you about the railways and how they were first built?

I did. I know it's not a girly thing to want to know about but I thought it was really interesting. I had even asked to look it all up in one of the grown-up library books. And that's how

I found out that even though my dad is a really brainy scientist, he's not very good at getting things like dates in the right order. When I read the grown-up book, I realised that he had told me a load of stuff that wasn't quite right.

But I didn't tell him, I didn't mind. I didn't want to be a smarty-pants.

Laura always said that I was special. She said she loved my magic memory, but it seemed that no one at school liked it so perhaps it's not so cool to know lots of things. Maybe it's not so great that I can remember everything.

DAD: Do you remember who Robert Stephenson was?

I closed my eyes and remembered the book. I saw page number forty-five. There was a black and white picture of a funny-looking train and two men wearing strange clothes and top hats. I saw the page as if it was right in front of me but I didn't say a word.

DAD: Emma?

I looked up to him and smiled. Dad wouldn't laugh. Dad wouldn't mind.

ME: George and his son Robert Stephenson built the first ever steam locomotive in 1829.
DAD: I love that you can do that! I wish I had your brain! You're a very lucky girl.

I loved it when he smiled like that because it reminded me of Laura's smile. And sometimes when my mum did her silly laugh she sounded a bit like Laura too. It was like even though Laura was gone, she'd left little pieces of herself everywhere.

We walked along the tow path in silence. Dad called it a 'comfortable silence', he said that there weren't many people in the world that you could sit in a room with or walk down the street with and not feel the need to say a thing. I sort of knew what he meant because even though Laura was such a chatterbox that teachers were always having to tell her off, even though you could usually only ever hear her voice in the playground, when we were on our own in our bedroom, when she was lying on her bed colouring and I was lying on my bed reading, she was as quiet as a mouse. Every so often she would just look over to me and smile. 'Just checking,' she'd say, 'Just checking that you're still there.' Comfortable silences, we were good at those.

The tow path seemed to go on for ever and every now and then we had to go underneath a little bridge. Some of the bridges were so low you almost had to duck to get under them. On one side of the path were lots of fields and in the distance I saw a train go by. On the other side everything kept changing: there was a grubby old building, the back of a pub where two men were shouting at each other, a shop which had graffiti all down the side of it and a little house which had every window smashed. We went past a really tall block of flats and at the very top I saw someone hanging out their washing. The tow path was quite busy. I saw lots of people walking their dogs, some people running and quite a lot of people on bicycles.

After a while things started looking a bit greener and I noticed that there were some houses right by the canal. Dad called them the 'really posh' houses. When I looked at them again I noticed that they were all very big and they didn't have a little patch of concrete for a garden like we did. Instead they all had long grassy lawns with lots of flowers and tall trees and some of the gardens came all the way down to the water.

We had to sort of creep under the next little bridge and that is when I saw them. In the canal, lined up like Rory's tiny train set, were lots of different, very long, very narrow little boats. They were kind of parked in the water and as we walked past the first one I saw that they really did have a sort of house plonked on top. I looked into the distance and saw boat after boat after boat. And every single one was different.

The first one was painted bright red and its little windows had stripy curtains. The second one was much bigger and it had a crooked black chimney with smoke chugging out of it. Houseboat followed houseboat, but my favourite was painted purple and silver. I bent down and I tried to look inside but I realised that the windows weren't made of glass, they were made of large shiny mirrors. So I just ended up staring at my own reflection, looking at my stupid, sticky-uppy hair. And then I heard a loud booming voice and two wellington boots appeared on the tow path in front of me.

LOUD BOOMING VOICE: Hullo!

I looked up at the loud-booming-voice-man and I watched Dad put down our bags and the two of them hugged each other.

DAD: Come and give Grandpa a hug then.

I looked at Grandpa and he looked at me.

GRANDPA: Aha! Weighing me up, are you?

Weighing him? I looked him up and down again. I looked at his scruffy trousers and his crumpled green and blue checkered shirt.

ME: But . . . but . . . I'm not very good at weighing. Miss Cauber says I always get the kilograms mixed up with the grams.

For some reason this made Grandpa laugh loudly and he bent down to look right at me.

His hair was thick and curly, just like my dad's, and his eyes were darkest blue, just like my dad's. And when he smiled again I realised that they were almost identical, although Grandpa had lots and lots of creases on his face and his hair was almost white, not black like my dad's.

Just at that moment we heard the sound of church bells, and I suddenly remembered the worst ever day. The worst and most horrid day that has ever been and ever will be. I remembered the other church again. I remembered sitting next to Grandpa in the car on the way back home. I remember getting snotty tears on the collar of his black jacket. Everyone was wearing black. I remembered again and I didn't want to.

Suddenly I felt really horrible, almost sick and I thought I was going to cry so I just stared at my feet. No one said anything and then Grandpa held out his hand to me. I looked down at it and then up to his face. He was smiling at me kindly.

GRANDPA: Why don't we start again? I'm really happy to see you, Emma.

He held out his hand once more and this time I shook it.

GRANDPA: Good! I forgot – you're one of us. Another Lefty!

I looked up at Dad with an 'I-don't-understand-you-grown-ups' look and Dad held up his left hand and wriggled it in the air.

DAD: Left-handed, silly. You're left-handed. Like me. Like Grandpa. We're all Lefties.

That was one of the few things that *was* different about Laura and me. She was right-handed and I am left-handed. I've never liked being left-handed. At school I have to use 'special' scissors and when we're working, when I'm trying to write, I always get someone else's elbow poking into my arm so that my writing gets all smudged. I didn't like being left-handed. I didn't like that I was different to Laura. I didn't like being left-handed until now.

Grandpa picked up my bag and pointed to the houseboat.

GRANDPA: This, my gorgeous granddaughter, is your home for the next three days.

Gorgeous? No one had ever called me that before. I was always Laura's sister. I was always 'the other twin'. I looked up at Grandpa and smiled *my* biggest smile.

GRANDPA: And look at that! See that smile! They're identical, aren't they?

Dad tilted his head to one side and looked back at me.

DAD: Yeah, I suppose they are.

Of course Grandpa would compare me to Laura . . . I started to get that funny feeling again when Grandpa bent down and looked right into my eyes.

GRANDPA: You look just like my mother. That smile. Those dimples. Just like your great-grandmother, Joy. She was one of the most wonderful people in the world, Joy – just like her name.

And I knew in that moment that this might only be my home for three nights, but I already wanted to stay for ever.

*

Have you ever been on a houseboat? I hope one day you do because it is a place like no other. When you walk around, it kind of moves about a little and inside everything is made much smaller which is perfect when you're just titchy, like me, although Grandpa and Dad looked really funny inside it. They looked like giants or something; they looked like they had grown too big or that the houseboat had shrunk around them.

Grandpa took my bag and showed me to my bedroom. It was only big enough for a teeny bed which was tucked up against the side of the room. There was a small shelf above the bed that was filled with photographs. I saw one of my dad when he was a small boy sitting inside a tractor, there were two of me and Laura and a black and white photograph of an older women. She had a sort of familiar face and pinned to the collar of her blouse was a broach with the letters J K.

I peered out of the small round window and saw that it had just started to rain. I looked around at the little room and decided that even though there was just enough space for one person, I thought it was the most perfect bedroom that I had ever been in. Apart from the smell, that is. I was just trying to work out what it was when Grandpa bent down and, from underneath the bed, pulled out a very stinky pair of socks.

GRANDPA: Oh, sorry about that. I expect these haven't *ever* seen a washing machine!

Even better, I thought, *there's no one here to moan about all the washing they have to do.*

While Dad went out to get us a Chinese takeaway, Grandpa gave me the grand tour, which didn't take long. In fact, I counted that it was only twenty-five steps from one end of the houseboat to the other end. There was a bathroom, my room, Grandpa's bedroom and in the main part of the boat there was a sort of kitchen with a little table and two benches. All along the side of the boat were rectangular-shaped windows that looked out on to the canal. I sat down on one of the bench seats.

GRANDPA: Those turn into a bed. That's where your dad will sleep tonight.

I looked down at the benches and couldn't imagine how *they* could turn into a bed like some kind of Transformer. But after we had eaten our dinner (and I had stuffed my face with the most delicious little pancakes and bits of crispy duck), I cleaned my teeth and washed my face in the smallest bathroom in the entire world and then grandpa showed me how the benches turned into a bed. One minute there were two bench seats and the next minute it was a bed! I stood watching in amazement because it seemed to me as though my grandpa had performed some kind of furniture magic.

ME: Wow! That's really cool. Can't I sleep here?

He shook his head and laughed.

GRANDPA: Not tonight, but maybe next time if Rory comes to visit too you can sleep out here instead.

I thought about that for a second and I decided that I didn't want Rory to ever come here. This was *my* new, special place. I folded my arms and frowned.

ME: Rory still wets the bed.

Grandpa looked at me with squinty eyes, picked up his mug and ruffled my hair.

GRANDPA: Okey-dokey. Just us then. But now, my gorgeous granddaughter with the perfect dimples, it's time for bed and if you're really lucky, I'll read you a bedtime story.

I ran back to bed, pulled up the duvet and waited. I couldn't remember the last time anyone had ever actually read to me. I always, always just read to myself.

When Grandpa finally came in he sat down at the end of my bed and in his hands was an old-looking book that even I had never seen before. It was called *Tom Flemming and the Painted Sea*. On the cover was a picture of a huge sailing boat and standing high up on one of the sails was a boy with an eye patch. I was just about to tell Grandpa about Lexi when he put on a tiny pair of glasses and opened the book. From the moment he read the first sentence, I was out at sea with Tom Flemming on his magical boat; I could smell the salty sea air, I could hear the sound of the seagulls and even though I was scared of heights, it was me that climbed the main sail. I could almost feel the wind in my sticky-uppy hair.

*

The next morning, it was my dad that had sticky-uppy hair and he smelt like the bottom of an anchor. He was still lying in his magic furniture bed when I came for breakfast.

ME: Phew! Why do you look like that, Dad?

He pulled the cover up over his head and groaned.

GRANDPA: Your dad had a bit of a late night.

Grandpa handed me a glass of orange juice.

GRANDPA: Your dad has got a *hangover*, hasn't he?

Dad groaned and when I looked at his face I thought that he looked kind of ill.

GRANDPA: Your dad's not feeling too good, are you, James?!

Grandpa seemed to be talking very loudly all of a sudden.

ME: Will you have to go to bed early tonight then?

Grandpa turned to me and laughed.

GRANDPA: I think that is a very good idea. And I think that your dad can stay here today, as he really doesn't look very well. So what shall we do? What would *you* like to do, Emma?

I didn't know what to say. I looked around at the houseboat and my stinky, groaning dad.

ME: Can we go out? Can we go and explore?

11

My first day in Oxford began with a wobble. We set off to explore, but the first thing I had to do was to learn how to ride a grown-up bike without crashing. Grandpa had two bikes and leant me one to ride. I found it hard to change gears, cycle in a straight line, watch out for the other people *and* try very hard *not* to look over the edge of the tow path into the canal. It was pretty hard to do all of that at the same time.

When my helmet slipped down across my eyes, I crashed into the back of Grandpa's bike and the two of us collapsed in a heap by the side of a little bridge. But he wasn't cross or anything and it didn't hurt much, so we just lay on the tow path giggling.

GRANDPA: Don't you have a bike to ride at home?

I picked up my bike and tightened the strap on my helmet.

ME: Mum says they're too dangerous.

We climbed back on to our bikes.

GRANDPA: Well, this is Oxford and nearly everyone uses a bike to get around.

We cycled over the bridge, past rows of little houses and when we turned left I saw what he meant. There *were* lots of people on bikes. Loads and loads!

There were people on racing bikes and people on mountain bikes, but there were also quite a lot that were on bikes just like my grandpa's. They *all* had handlebars that curved in towards you and a sort of shopping basket at the front. I saw one woman with a loaf of bread in hers and a man with a pair of trainers sticking out of his, but the best one was a much, much older lady who wasn't wearing a helmet like you're supposed to – instead she was wearing a large straw hat. The brim of the hat was decorated with lots of colourful flowers and in her basket was a tiny, fluffy white dog. As she cycled past me I saw that its tongue was hanging out and its front paws were sort of gripping the top of the basket. It looked like it was saying, 'Faster, Granny! Faster!' *Rascoe would love to do that*, I thought. Although, he's a bit of a porky old thing, so we'd need to find a bike that had a very large shopping trolley at the front instead of a little basket!

Every so often we had to stop and get off our bikes so that Grandpa could tell me what all the different buildings were. I know I was supposed to be listening, but I kept looking out for other bikes and I wondered if I'd get to see another little dog in a basket. I followed Grandpa down a little alleyway where we parked our bikes outside a special kind of cake shop. I took my helmet off and peered in through the window which was lit up with tiny pink and white lights. My eyes widened. I had seen all the cakes at my dad's favourite bakery before but nothing quite like this: doughnuts, cupcakes, teacakes, lemon drizzle, chocolate muffins, custard slices too, with frosting, butter cream, chocolate sprinkes, jam, cream and every colour icing you could think of! There were some that I had never seen before.

And I was allowed to choose anything I wanted. There were so many to choose from, and because I couldn't make up my mind, Grandpa said we could be really greedy.

GRANDPA: Let's be greedy gobblers, eh, shall we? Just like your dad used to be when he was your age. We can have as many as we want!

We didn't talk about anything for ages. It's a bit tricky to talk when your mouth is full of custard slice, jammy doughnut and apple danish. And it's even trickier to talk when you're munching on the best thing you've ever eaten and trying to work out the answer to lots of different questions in your head, like, what would my mum think of the mountain of cakes and when can I leave home and come and live with Grandpa?

After our cake feast, Grandpa took me to an enormous museum. I pretended to be interested in the bits of rock, fossils and all the dinosaurs, because I didn't want to tell Grandpa that my dad had shown me all of it before. I didn't want to tell him that after Laura died and Mum didn't stop crying, Dad used to take me and Rory out for the day. Sometimes we went to the cinema or bowling, but there were lots of times when he would just take me to the Natural History Museum, the zoo, M-Shed, the Planetarium or, my favourite place, At-Bristol. He said it would 'get us out of the house for a bit' but 'a bit' always turned into ages and we often spent hours wandering around with Dad telling me what this fossil was, what that rock was and what every dinosaur was called. I didn't really mind, but it seemed a bit weird to me that while my mum was sitting at home crying over my dead sister, we were spending hours and hours staring at lots of dead things.

When we got back to Grandpa's houseboat, my dad announced that he would do all the cooking, but as I had never ever seen him with an apron on, I watched in fits of giggles as he spilt the sauce, burnt a pan and dropped a bag of frozen peas all over the floor.

After dinner we all sat at the little table playing Scrabble. Every so often I looked out of one of the little rectangular windows across the canal. The rain had stopped and the sky was so clear that I could see the moon reflecting off the water. When we'd finished eating, my dad read to me and stroked my sticky-uppy hair until I fell fast asleep. It was a perfect day.

*

The next day was our last day at Grandpa's but no one was ready to do anything until it was almost lunchtime. It wasn't like our house where everyone was always rushing around and banging things about. There was no grumping and groaning. There was no moodiness and moaning. There was no pretending to be happy or pretending not to be sad. There were no tears or tantrums. There was none of all that. It was peaceful. It was perfect, as we all just padded around the houseboat in our pyjamas.

I read more of *Tom Flemming*, Dad read something about Mars, and Grandpa sat at the little table with his tiny computer.

ME: What you doing?
GRANDPA: Emailing someone. I've just finished writing about a walking holiday I went on in North Africa so now I have to send it to the person in charge of the newspaper. It's a bit like handing in your homework.

Dad laughed. Years ago, when my dad was a teenager, Grandpa used to get up very early every morning, put on a suit and tie and take the train to London. He worked at the very top of one of the tallest buildings in the very best office in all of London. Then he would spend all day every day

99

telling people what to do and what not to do. Telling people what to buy and what not to buy. Dad says it made Grandpa rich, but he was really, really miserable. So miserable that he left his office one Thursday afternoon, threw his tie off London Bridge, got on the train to Oxford and never went back to London again. Now his office is wherever he wants it to be and it seems to me that he doesn't have to do anything if he doesn't really want to.

He looked up and waved at me to come and sit beside him.

GRANDPA: Look, I'm on a thing called Hotmail.

Hotmail? Why did I know that? I tried to think . . .

ME: What's that?

He took off his glasses and looked at me with a sort of surprised look.

GRANDPA: Do you mean to tell me that your sixty-five-year-old grandpa knows more about computers than you?

I suddenly felt embarrassed.

GRANDPA: James – you've got the internet at home, haven't you?

My dad put down his book and sighed.

DAD: Of course we do, Dad, but The Dragon wants them to learn everything the old-fashioned way.

I knew exactly who The Dragon was. It was Dad's horrid name for Mum. The name he sometimes used when they were arguing, and I didn't like it. Grandpa didn't either. He looked really serious and turned to my dad and spoke a bit like Mrs Cauber does when she's telling Josh and Merrick off.

GRANDPA: Hey, young man. Name calling? I don't remember ever teaching you that. I don't want to hear that ever again. Fi is like a daughter to me so I don't ever want to hear you making childish, hurtful comments like that, especially in front of your children. Do you hear?

Dad's cheeks went bright red and he kind of nodded. He looked a bit like Rory did when Mum told him off for squeezing the toothpaste all around the toilet seat. It was kind of funny to see my dad get properly told off by another grown up.

ME: If Mum is . . . you know, a dragon, what are you, dad?

Grandpa laughed.

DAD: The princess locked up in the tower?

We all laughed and I suddenly had an image of my dad in a floaty, pink princess costume.

Then Grandpa explained everything about emails and email addresses to me. It's not like I hadn't ever heard of it all before, but I'd never really been interested until now. I decided I wanted my own email address so we tried to set up an account for me but it seemed that I have a very popular name. We tried all sort of versions but they'd *all* been taken by some other girl which just reminded me of how dull and boring my name really is. After a while the computer made a few suggestions for addresses that I could have. We scrolled down the list and eventually Grandpa pointed at one of them.

GRANDPA: That's the one! That's just the ticket. In fact, that was my nickname when I was at school.

I looked at the address: EddieE@hotmail.com. Eddie? I looked up at Grandpa.

GRANDPA: At my school everyone was called by their last name and in my form there were two of us called Edwards. In the end, everyone just called me Eddie.

Grandpa explained how it all worked, he showed me how I could log in and out of my inbox, and how to set my password and that the little yellow envelopes meant I had a message. I sat there staring at the screen for a while but I didn't have anyone to send an email to. Then I remembered what I'd seen on the last day of school. I did know an email address! I could send an email to Lexi. I had loads and *loads* of things I wanted to ask her. But this time I wouldn't say anything about her patch and as she wasn't even in the same room as me I couldn't make the mistake of gawping at her like an idiot.

I sat there for ages staring at the screen and when Grandpa came back I had only typed in the address.

GRANDPA: Lexi? Is she a friend from school?

So I told him all about Lexi. I told him how I had met her on the way to school. I told him how she had made friends with lots of other girls and how she had the same birthday as my new birthday. I told him that there was something different about her, like I sort of knew her but I didn't. I told him that one day when I had been upset she sort of tried to help but I never knew what the cool thing was to say, like all the other girls . . . like Laura. I felt the tears run down my cheeks.

Grandpa didn't say anything for a while. He pulled out a handkerchief from his jeans pocket, wiped my tears away and in a really quiet voice I told him that I had done a bit of staring, that I had done quite a *lot* of staring. And no matter how hard I tried, I always seemed to say the stupidest things and that I couldn't help but want to know why Lexi wore an eye patch.

Grandpa took a deep breath and looked very thoughtful.

GRANDPA: Why don't we start with something short and simple?

So, my first ever email was very short and very simple.

To: Lexiland@hotmail.com
From: EddieE@hotmail.com
Hi Lexi,
I'm having a great Easter holiday, are you?
Emma

12

As it was our last day, we all went out so that Dad could show me the house where he had grown up. He showed me the school he had gone to and then a special college where he'd met Mum. We stopped at the entrance to an old building and Dad put his hand on one of the large wooden doors.

DAD: This is where I first laid eyes on your mum. This is the exact spot where she dropped all her books and practically knocked me over at the same time.
ME: And what did you do then?

Laura and I used to love hearing stories about when Mum and Dad were younger, and once Mum went up to the attic and brought down a box full of old photographs of them when they were at university. We had laughed and laughed when we saw Mum's *really* big hair and Dad in his clown trousers. He always looked funny in old pictures, like someone had tipped him upside down and shaken him really hard. But there were loads of pictures where Mum looked as though she had asked Rory to choose all of her clothes.

DAD: What did I do? What did I do after your mum came crashing into me?

Grandpa laughed.

GRANDPA: He probably blushed like a beetroot, picked up all of her books and said sorry.

Dad sighed and looked down at me again.

DAD: That is *exactly* what I did. I was a bit shy, you know. I used to not really know what to say to girls, especially one as pretty as your mum.
GRANDPA: What do you mean 'used to'? You're still not very good at it!

Dad laughed and Grandpa pushed open the door. I thought it was a bit like the entrance to a castle and standing by the doorway was a little man in a funny-hat. Dad and Grandpa talked to him for ages until eventually the little man went back into his office and when he came back he brought with him a very large, old-looking key. Dad took my hand and we walked out of the hallway straight into a garden. A garden right in the middle of a building! I'd never seen a garden like it before. The building sort of fitted perfectly around it. It looked to me as though every blade of grass was exactly the same length – as though it had been painted green that very morning. We walked round the garden, along a path, through a stone archway and up a spiral staircase. It really was like being in a castle.

We stopped in front of another wooden door and Dad took the old key and unlocked the door with a loud clunking sound. I stepped inside and looked around the room. The walls didn't have wallpaper or paint or anything like that. They were all covered in a beautiful, honey-coloured wood. It even smelt like Grandma's log basket.

On one side of the room was an enormous bookcase with shelves and shelves of books. There were large leather books like the Bible, tiny books with orange spines. Some of them had numbers, roman numerals or strange-looking letters. On the other side of the room there were three pretty-shaped windows with a large desk in front of them and when I walked towards it, I realised that you could see down to the lovely square garden.

So for a couple of hours, I forgot all about the email I sent and when we got back to the houseboat it was so late and I was so tired that I fell asleep without thinking to check my inbox.

That night I dreamt I was in a houseboat which had

shelves and shelves of books but Laura was cycling along the tow path and in her basket was an enormous stripy green cake.

*

When we said goodbye to Grandpa the next day, he told me he would send me an email every week and that he would definitely see me again in the summer holidays. Grandpa let me borrow *Tom Flemming and the Painted Sea* and gave me a second book about Tom too. As Dad and I walked back towards the car, I decided that I couldn't wait until we could come back to Oxford and stay with Grandpa in his perfect little houseboat.

<u>In the car on the way home</u>

DAD: Did you have a good time?

ME: The bestest! Grandpa is the bestest! How could anyone not love Grandpa?

Dad turned to me and frowned.

DAD: What makes you say that?

I thought about it for a second and at first I wasn't sure I knew why I'd said it, but then I remembered that I'd once heard Grandma say that she 'didn't like him very much'.

ME: Grandma doesn't really like him.

108

DAD: She doesn't dislike him. They just can't agree on anything. Your Grandma is very, very . . . Mum's mum is very, very . . .

ME: Bossy?

He laughed and turned the radio down.

DAD: Yes, she is quite bossy. The thing is your Grandma likes rules. You know, she likes to do everything just right, just so. She's very neat and tidy. She's always on time. She's very organised. And my dad, your Grandpa is more . . .

I thought about Grandpa and the socks that hadn't been washed, the cake feast that Mum would have never let me gobble down and how no matter what he wore, he always looked a bit crumpled. Whereas I once saw my grandma ironing a pair of knickers.

DAD: They are just very different. You know, Grandma used to be a head teacher and Grandpa once lived in a tepee.

ME: A tepee! Really? Like the American Indians? Why?

DAD: Because he wanted to know what it was like. He was going to write about it and he needed to know what it felt like to go to sleep and wake up in a tepee. So he tried it out and it felt really good.

ME: For how long?

DAD: Till it started raining everyday!

ME: And did he write about it?

Dad smiled at me again.

DAD: He did indeed. In one of his books. And one day, when you're older, you'll probably read all about it for yourself.

I sat back and closed my eyes. I knew Grandpa spent a lot of time travelling around and then writing about it, but I just thought he stayed in hotels and that sort of thing. I didn't know he stayed in tepees or anything like that and I hoped that one day I could do the very same thing.

13

When we got back home, I ran into the kitchen to find Mum. I couldn't wait to tell her all about the houseboat and the adventures we'd had with Grandpa, but Mum wasn't in the mood for listening at all. When I told her all about the bikes and how me and Grandpa had raced up and down the tow path, she started telling Dad off. She said things like 'James, what did we talk about? What did I say to you before you left?' And when I butted in and told her that *everyone* uses a bike in Oxford, she just asked me lots of weird questions about whether it was hard work, and if I felt out of breath.

Then when I unpacked my suitcase, Mum complained about all the washing she had to do now we were back and she moaned at Dad for not helping with Rory. She even grumbled at me when she saw that it had been me who had taken Laura's old rabbit because Rory had been looking for it all day. But that made me really cross so I got up from the table and said, 'It isn't Rory's Rabbit. It was Laura's so, really, it belongs to me. ME!' I sort of shouted the last bit but Mum just shook her head and sighed.

MUM: But what if you'd taken it all the way to Oxford and left it there? What if you'd lost it?

And I wanted to say this: 'If I had left it on Grandpa's houseboat, if Laura's old rabbit got to stay in Oxford with Grandpa it would probably be much happier anyway.' But I didn't say anything. Instead I just stomped upstairs to bed and when Mum knocked on the door to say goodnight, I shouted, 'JUST LEAVE ME ALONE!'

*

As I lay in bed that night, all I could think about was how Mum and Dad were always fighting. I wondered if they would get divorced like Greta's parents and I decided that if they did I would definitely, definitely want to live with my dad.

VOICE: No, you wouldn't

I lay really still.

VOICE: You wouldn't want to *just* live with Dad. He can't even cook.

I thought about the food Dad had tried to cook for Grandpa and me with burnt sauce and peas all over the floor. Then I thought of Mum's yummy mashed potatoes and the chocolate pudding she used to make for me and Laura.

ME: Mum seems to have forgotten how to cook. She seems to have forgotten to do loads of things.

There was a little sigh and I waited.

VOICE: Well, you're the one with the magic memory. Why don't you remind her?

*

The rest of the Easter holidays were boring. I only got two Easter eggs and one of those was dark chocolate, but every day I sent Grandpa an email and he sent me one too, but nothing came from LexiLand. Not one single email. Every time I logged on to check I sort of held my breath, closed my eyes and even crossed my fingers too, but there was nothing. For some reason that made me feel quite funny, a little bit sort of angry, and by the time I was packing my bag to go back to school I decided not to care about Lexi any more. I didn't care about her and her stupid Lexiland.

14

The first day back at school was dull. The second day back was *really* dull. But on the third day, two strange things happened. After morning-break, Lexi put her hand up.

MISS CAUBER: Yes, Lexi, what is it?

Lexi sort of frowned at her and said nothing. She looked really confused.

LEXI: Is it Tuesday today?

The rest of the class sniggered. It was the second time she'd asked what day it was that lesson.

Then, at lunch-break, I was sitting by the sports hut when

I heard a loud shouting. In the far corner by the fire escape was a crowd of girls and boys from my class. Erin was crying and Greta and Lexi were shouting at each other. I heard something about a sleepover and I stood up and walked closer so that I could hear what was going on. Then the shouting got even louder and Greta yelled, 'Well, my mum says it's no wonder you've got problems. I don't care if you wear a stupid eye patch!'

I don't know why but Greta was getting meaner and nastier with every day. I watched Lexi move so close to Greta that her nose was almost touching hers.

LEXI: And I don't care if your mum is on the telly looks just like a . . .

But I didn't hear what Lexi said because Mrs McWatter appeared in the playground and took Lexi with her. I didn't think Lexi's patch was stupid at all. It was cool. It was, well, I don't really know what, but I knew one thing for sure: Greta the Great was not so great any more.

After lunch Lexi didn't come back to class and Miss Cauber just gave us a really boring lecture about name calling and being kind to each other. She even read out a story which was supposed to have a moral or something, but I wasn't really listening.

When I got home from school I checked my inbox and even though there wasn't anything from Lexi, I decided that I would send her another message to see if she was OK.

To: Lexiland@hotmail.com

From: EddieE@hotmail.com

Hi,

I don't think your patch is stupid. It's cool but thanks to you I had to listen to the world's most boring lecture from Miss C about name calling. Apparently name calling isn't allowed at St Thomas. Do you think she knows that everyone calls her Coffee-breath Cauber?

E

Lexi wasn't in school for the rest of the week, and I kept checking my inbox to see if she had sent me a message back. But it was empty every time.

I even checked my inbox three times on Sunday morning, but then we had to go to Grandma's house for lunch and by the time we got back Mum said I wasn't allowed to go on the computer. This made me really mad so I slammed the kitchen door and the living room door, and as I went upstairs I stamped up every single step. I did it so hard that it hurt my feet a bit. I tried to slam the bathroom door, but that door doesn't shut properly so I ended up just stamping around the bathroom instead. At one point, I even kicked the laundry basket over and then I realised that this was just how Rory behaved and I felt sort of stupid.

But I *was* cross, I was really angry and I could feel my heart beat really quickly again, like it did the time I shouted at Miss Cauber. I was so busy banging around in the bathroom that I didn't hear my dad come up the stairs. He stuck his head around the door.

DAD: Are you quite finished in there? I'm not sure you've woken up the whole neighbourhood, but if I join in perhaps we can wake them up together?

I suddenly had a picture in my head of both Dad and I jumping and stomping around the bathroom like a pair of tap-dancing elephants which kind of made me giggle. Dad smiled.

<u>At bedtime</u>

VOICE: Do your feet hurt?

ME: A little. They sort of sting a bit.

VOICE: Idiot.

ME: Was Greta always so horrible?

VOICE: I thought you were the one with the magic memory. She used to come here after school until . . .

I thought about it for second and I suddenly remembered. When Rory was a baby, Mum didn't go to work so she always picked us up from school and Greta sometimes came with us. She'd sometimes stay at our house until her mum was finished filming her television show.

ME: Yeah, but her mum was always really late and then one time she just forgot to pick her up and it was almost midnight before she came and . . .

117

VOICE: And Greta was crying and crying because she thought her mum had left her but . . .

ME: But her mum didn't say sorry or anything. She didn't even cuddle her or anything.

Neither of us said anything for ages.

ME: Laura?

Silence.

ME: I still miss you.

Now that it was April, it was time for a Big Change, which meant that instead of Mum going to work a little bit, she had to go every day. So I had a choice: after-school club or Grandma's house. On Monday morning over breakfast, Mum asked me what I wanted to do.

MUM: It's up to you. You know Grandma loves having you and Rory to stay, but if you'd rather stay with your friends at school, then she doesn't mind at all.

I thought about it for a nanosecond. Staying a minute longer in school with a bunch of people like Josh and Greta or go to my Grandma's house? It was what my dad called a 'no brainer' – which means that I didn't even need to think about it at all.

Dad handed me a glass of juice and a tablet.

DAD: Down the hatch.

I gulped down the pill and juice and I turned to Mum and smiled.

ME: It's a no-brainer, Mum. Grandma's!

Mum smiled and told me to go the toilet, put on my shoes and coat so we could walk to school. But when I came out into the hall I saw the new shoes again and my stomach flipped over.

Mum must have found where I'd hidden them in the cupboard. Stupid new shoes.

I sat down on Rory's little stool and looked down at the black school shoes. They were ugly. They were size *two*. A whole size bigger than my last pair. For the first time my feet were bigger than Laura's.

I sort of stared at them for ages and when Dad shouted from the kitchen to get a move on I stood up and kicked the left shoe down the hall. Then I turned and kicked the right one up in the air. It sort of shot over Rascoe's head, bounced off the toilet door and I watched in horror as it spun backwards into the toilet, landing with a loud splash. Fortunately I had flushed the toilet. Unfortunately Rascoe thought the whole thing was bit of a game and before I had a chance to stop him, he'd jumped up out of his basket, run across the hall and, with his fluffy brown tail wagging this way and that way, he went to retrieve the shoe.

It wouldn't have been so bad if he hadn't knocked a toilet roll into the toilet at the same time. It wouldn't have been so bad if he hadn't just come back indoors covered in muddy puddle water. And it definitely wouldn't have been so bad if both Mum and Dad hadn't appeared in the hall in their clean and very smart work clothes at the exact same time that Rascoe's head popped up from inside the toilet.

For a second they didn't move, neither did I, but Rascoe, who was very pleased indeed with his little toilet trophy, came bounding up to Mum, dropped the soggy shoe on the toe of her boot and before we had a chance to move out of the way, he shook himself all over us.

MUM: For God's sake!

I looked up at her suit. It was covered in brown droplets.

ME: Sorry.
MUM: For once, would you just do as you're told? Could you? I have enough to do. I have enough to do without this sort of nonsense, Emma! *Really!* Just look at my suit, will you?

Dad looked pretty angry too. The important work papers he'd been writing on at breakfast had been sprayed with

120

water and I could see the ink begin to run down the page as he tried desperately to blot them dry with his jacket sleeve.

DAD: Emma, just put your other shoes on, will you? We're all going to be late now.

On the way to school Mum asked me loads of questions: *How was I feeling? How did I sleep? Did I feel tired? Did walking up the steep hill feel easy or hard?* She was always asking me questions like this. It was really annoying because the answer was always the same. *I am fine. I slept fine. I do not feel tired and walking up the steep hill is always a bit hard because it is really, really steep.* She was obviously still cross with me, because she didn't kiss me goodbye at the school gates. Even Rory looked up to me and said, 'Naughty noodle.' I felt really bad as I watched her and Rory run down the street together.

By the time I got to my classroom I was starting to feel a bit nervous. What if Lexi *had* read my emails and thought they were really stupid? What if she had made friends with Greta again, told her all about it and they were laughing at me? But Lexi wasn't even in school.

She wasn't in school the next day or the day after that. In fact, Lexi wasn't at school for the whole week. Miss Cauber didn't say why and no one seemed to know. I even heard Greta say she was pleased that Lexi wasn't in school and she hoped that she never came back.

Well, what she actually said was 'Good riddance to bad rubbish' and it seemed to me that she said it in a particularly nasty, I-talk-like-I've-got-a-peg-on-my-nose kind of a way.

I couldn't check my email after school all that week because Grandma doesn't have the internet and when I got home Mum always told me that it was too late.

Then my mum took me to Aunt Shelly's for the whole weekend so I forgot all about checking my email.

I especially forgot about it when we all stayed up late and Aunt Shelly played the film *Mamma Mia* really loudly – so loudly that the grumpy man that lived upstairs kept banging on the floor to tell us to turn it down but Mum and Aunt Shelly just sang along even louder. They danced around the tiny living room until Mum kicked a glass of red wine all over the carpet. I thought Aunt Shelly would be really cross, but she didn't mind at all. She didn't shout or anything, she just giggled and said, 'Just as well the head teacher isn't here!' Mum and her laughed and laughed about it until they both had tears rolling down their cheeks and Aunt Shelly's make-up sort of slid down her face.

When Mum put me to bed I asked her what Aunt Shelly had meant.

MUM: Well, Grandma was a head teacher, remember? One time, when Shelly was about your age, I was supposed to be babysitting whilst Grandma was giving someone a piano lesson – well, my naughty little sister thought that it would be a brilliant idea to do a bit of painting. Anyway, Grandma was not best pleased to find red handprints all over her new curtains . . .

But Mum stopped suddenly. I watched her hand go up to her mouth and I could see she had almost-tears in her eyes. She didn't say anything for a while and I wondered if she had done the same thing as me. I wondered if she had thought of Laura too. Laura and the 'Paint Pot Disaster'. Laura hadn't meant to make such a mess and she hadn't known that the paint was the sort that didn't wash off. I was pretty sure that Mum and I were both thinking of Laura and the white-painted footprints that she had danced all over the kitchen, the garden and the living room carpet.

I watched Mum wipe a tear from her cheek. I saw her gulp and try really hard, but in the end she ran out of the room sobbing and I thought that perhaps I was the one who made everything worse.

*

On Monday Lexi was back in school. Every so often I looked over at her seat and tried to smile at her but she was always gazing out of the window.

At the end of the day, I waited at the gates for Lexi to come out, but Grandma was in such a rush to get back for the washing machine repairman that she sort of ran-walked me all the way back to the car. She drove a bit too fast over the bridge and I don't think she was really concentrating, because she almost missed the turning to her little house.

Grandma's house doesn't have an upstairs, but it does have a pretty garden that goes all the way around it with a pond with lots of different coloured fish and an enormous vegetable patch at the bottom. When I go to Grandma's house, she fusses over me a bit like Mum does with Rory, but she can be really, really bossy.

It's still much better than after-school club, but most of the time she wants us to do things together. We do baking or gardening or working in the vegetable patch. Once we even had to clear out the garden shed. I hated that because it smelt funny and there were loads of massive spiders. Plus Grandma is always trying to tell me about things, like the names of different flowers or why some vegetables grow better than others or how old something is, which means that sometimes being at Grandma's house can be a little bit like school.

At Grandma's, in the big room with the telly

GRANDMA: How about a bit of piano practice?

I groaned. I like playing the piano but, well, it's kind of boring doing the same thing over and over and over again. Grandma says 'Practice makes perfect', but Laura used to say, 'Practising the same bit of music again and again makes me HATE the piece of music that I once really liked.'

I sat down at the piano, Grandma opened up the music book and I played. Well, I tried to play 'Raindrops Keep Falling On My Head', but I didn't really want to play, so I deliberately got it all wrong. I just bashed the keys a lot until it stopped sounding like raindrops and ended up sounding more like a hail storm instead.

GRANDMA: I would have thought that, with your photographic memory, you'd have memorised all the notes.

She was right, I knew exactly how. I'd known exactly how to play it properly from the first time I'd read it.

GRANDMA: How about you play it once for me nicely, and then you can watch the telly with some of the carrot cake that I made this morning?

Another 'no brainer'. So I played the piece of music again, only this time I played it perfectly. And afterwards I sat down in front of the telly and Grandma brought me a gigantic slice of my favourite carrot cake. I looked down at the sticky white frosting and my beady, greedy eyes lit up. Then, as I took a massive bite, Grandma looked down at me with a really, frowny face.

GRANDMA: Don't wolf it down in one go. Chew it slowly. Don't want you choking or anything.

I thought of Laura and our very last birthday party. It had been here in Grandma's garden. I suddenly remembered and when I swallowed the piece of delicious carrot cake I felt really sad again.

ME: Don't worry, Grandma, I'm not stupid enough to choke to death on a slice of silly cake.

Grandma turned around and quickly bent down to face me.

GRANDMA: What did you just say?

She looked funny, like she was angry, but also kind of shocked, as though I'd just shouted out all the really bad swear words that I know.

ME: I . . . won't . . . choke . . . I won't die . . . you know, like Laura. I won't choke on the cake.

Grandma stared right at me. She was sort of scaring me a bit. Then she shook her head and looked down at the floor. When she looked back up again, I could see that she was crying.

GRANDMA: Is that what you think happened?

What was she talking about? That's what *did* happen. I was there. It was *our* birthday and I was standing right next to Laura when it all happened.

I looked over Grandma's shoulder, through the window and into the garden. *I remember*, I thought, *it happened out there in your stupid garden.*

I was just about to say exactly that when I heard a car drive up. I looked out the window – it was Mum and Rory. Grandma ran to the door and let them in. Rory ran towards me and jumped up on to the sofa. Grandma whispered something to Mum and then they went into the kitchen and shut the door behind them. I couldn't hear what they were saying but after a while I heard my mum sort of shouting so I pushed Rory off my lap, ran to the door and listened.

The other side of the door

MUM: What do you mean 'lied to her'?

GRANDMA: She thinks her sister choked to death on a slice of birthday cake!

MUM: No, she doesn't.

GRANDMA: Fiona, I'm telling you, Emma thinks the birthday cake killed Laura! When are you going to tell her the truth?

The truth! What truth? What is the truth? What haven't I been told? What's going on?

15

We left Grandma's house in a rush and Mum had to wrestle with a screaming Rory who was having another tantrum. He screamed as Mum dragged him out of the door, he screamed when she fastened him into his little seat and in the end both Mum and I sang 'The Frog Song' to shut him up. Eventually he fell asleep so all we could hear were his little piglet snores. At the turning to our road Mum stopped the car.

MUM: Do you . . .

I waited.

MUM: Do you . . .

I waited again.

MUM: Do you . . . want to go for a pizza?

Pizza, I thought, *my favourite food in the whole world.*

ME: Oh! Yes! Can we go to *Danilo's* please?

Danilo's is the best pizza place in the world. It's only tiny and sometimes you even have to queue up to get a table. Laura loved going there but I couldn't remember the last time we'd been. I'd never been without Laura.

The best thing about *Danilo's*, apart from the pizza, is that you can draw on the tables. Well, you can draw on the table-cloth because they don't have ordinary ones, they have paper ones and in the middle of the table, next to the salt and pepper, there's a huge jug of crayons and pencils. So it doesn't matter if it takes ages for the pizza to arrive, because you can just draw all over the table cloth while you wait. Although Laura was the one who used to do all the drawing. She was the one who would draw lots of funny faces around the cutlery and the pepper pot. I just used to write our names in lots of different ways.

The pizza is so good that one time I didn't wait long enough for my slice to cool down before I ate it, and I burnt the roof of my mouth so badly that I had to suck on ice cubes to stop it from hurting. Laura had laughed at me, so I'd leant over to her and dropped an ice cube down her top. Then

Mum fished one out of her glass and popped one down my jumper and it wasn't long before there was a sort of silly ice-cube fight. Dad had laughed and said, 'You three girls! I can't take you anywhere.'

When we got to *Danilo's*, Mum settled Rory down with some crayons and when Maria the beautiful waitress came over, Mum ordered us all some drinks. Maria is Megan's mum and she sometimes comes into school to help out. As Maria wrote down the order, I looked up at her hair. Normally she wears it in a kind of bun on the top of her head, but today she was wearing it differently, so that it hung down below her shoulders in long, glossy black waves. I almost reached out to touch it.

MUM: So what did you do today, Emma?

There are lots of questions that Mum asks me, but that is the one question I really hate because it is completely stupid. It is even more stupid because she's a teacher so she knows exactly what we do all day.

MUM: Learn anything new?

I thought of what had happened at lunch-break when Josh kicked his football right over the wall and on to the road, and I wanted to say this: 'Yes, I learnt that if you say the "F" word really loudly, Miss Cauber will send you to sit outside Mrs McWatter's office.' But I didn't say it because Mum's phone rang and she got up from the table and walked over to the window to answer it.

Then Dad arrived. I jumped up from my seat, ran over to him and threw my arms around his waist.

DAD: That's a nice way to end a really horrible day at work.

Mum came back to the table and sat down.

MUM: That was your Aunt Shelly.

She looked up at Dad and shook her head.

MUM: I think she may have got on the wrong train or her train was cancelled. I couldn't really hear her. I don't know, there's always a drama with her.

Dad and I laughed. Aunt Shelly *was* always getting things mixed up. She once tried to make us dinner but she forgot to put the oven on. Another time she turned up for lunch a whole day early, and one day I went to the supermarket with her but she left her purse at home and then she locked us out of the car so we had to walk all the way back home without the shopping.

Finally the pizza arrived. It was delicious! I ate all of mine, some of Rory's and when we had dessert I got to eat a bit of Mum's tirama-something and a gigantic bowl of mint choco-late-chip ice-cream.

Laura always said it was the most disgusting flavour in the world, she said, 'Nothing that tastes like toothpaste should ever be mixed with chocolate.'

But it's my favourite.

As I scraped the last glob of melted ice-cream from my glass dish I kind of forgot. For a tiny moment I smiled, licked my lips and turned to see if Laura had finished hers too, but when I saw it was just Rory sitting next to me I just stared at him for a bit. It was really weird.

*

When Mum put Rory to bed she came into my bedroom and asked me to come downstairs. She said they wanted to talk to me about 'something'. I came down the stairs slowly. I didn't know what the 'something' was, but I hoped it wasn't as horrid as the 'something' I had made for the art corner.

I sat down opposite them. Mum was fiddling with her necklace and Dad kept rubbing the side of his head. They both looked really serious.

DAD: We need to talk to you about Laura.

I waited. I stared at the pattern on the rug and counted all the different shapes: diamonds, triangles, squares, circles. No one said anything. I waited. I turned the corner of the rug over with the tips of my toes. The colours were much brighter on the other side: reds, yellows, greens. I waited. The ice-cream started to churn around in my stomach.

132

ME: Am I in trouble?

DAD: No, of course not. You haven't done anything and you're not in trouble. Is that what you thought?

I looked up again. Dad was sort of frowning and Mum was picking at the skin around her nails. It was just like the time they came back from the hospital. It was just like the time they came back without Laura.

I felt my heart beat quicker. *Thud-thud. Thud-thud.* I decided that whatever it was they wanted to talk about, I didn't want to know. I wanted to put my hands to my ears to block out the sound of their voices. *Thud-thud. Thud-thud.*

Just at that moment I heard a loud squeaking noise and our front gate suddenly banged shut, then the doorbell rang. For a second no one moved then I ran to the door. When I saw who it was I jumped up, wrapped my arms around her neck and buried my face into her soft Rapunzel hair and breathed in her lovely lemony smell.

ME: Aunt Shelly!

AUNT SHELLY: Surprise!

Mum came into the hallway and when she saw who it was, she sort of laughed and sighed at the same time.

MUM: Missed your train home?

AUNT SHELLY: No. I got on the wrong train. Can you believe it? I got on the train going in the other direction.

Wrong platform. I was so tired. I had no idea. Just sat down, got my book out and . . . I only closed my eyes for a second . . . I would have ended up in Cornwall if the conductor hadn't woken me up. Can you imagine? So here I am in Bristol instead of London – just as well my favourite Sister lives here, isn't it?

I looked up at her and grinned, but then Mum looked a bit weird again, as though she was trying to work out a really, really hard sum. She sighed and leant against the door.

MUM: We were just about to . . . er . . . talk.

Mum and Aunt Shelly gave each other a funny look.

DAD: It can wait. Another time!
MUM: Come inside then, sis, it's freezing.

Aunt Shelly gave me her huge handbag and I ran inside.

AUNT SHELLY: So a sleepover on a school night?

I jumped up and ran to the stairs.

ME: Can she stay in my room? Please?

134

That night I lay awake for ages. I could hear Aunt Shelly, Mum and Dad talking downstairs really quietly. I wondered if they were talking about Laura.

My eyelids were just starting to close when Aunt Shelly crept into my bedroom. I turned on the snow globe.

AUNT SHELLY: Still awake?
ME: Yep.

She sat down on Laura's bed and took off her socks. Her toenails were painted a dark red colour. She pulled out a bottle of lotion and a ball of cotton wool from her handbag.

AUNT SHELLY: Time to take the gunk off.

I watched her wipe away her make-up. It seemed to take ages but I thought she looked much better without the 'gunk' and when she was finished she looked up at me and smiled again.

ME: Better!

She sort of laughed.

AUNT SHELLY: Oh, I don't know about that.
ME: No. Much better. Prettier than ever.

I lay back on my pillow and thought about the time that Laura and I had found Mum's old make-up bag. It was full of little bottles and boxes, lipsticks and brushes, shadows and powders and a sticky glossy thing that dripped everywhere. In the end, the two of us had just smeared red lipstick all over our cheeks so that we looked like Hiawatha.

AUNT SHELLY: I hear you're going to Grandma's house after school now. Are you having fun or is she making you 'do things'?

I laughed.

ME: Did she always make you do stuff when you were little?
AUNT SHELLY: *Always!* And when she wasn't making me, your mum did!
ME: Was Mum really, really bossy?
AUNT SHELLY: Yes! She used to tell me what to do and what not to do. What to play with and what not to play with until . . .

I grinned.

AUNT SHELLY: Until I had enough of being told what to do.
ME: Laura was always . . .

AUNT SHELLY: Yeah, she was just like your mum. Quite the bossy little thing, wasn't she?

I laughed again and turned on my side. I remembered one summer afternoon a couple of years ago when Mum and Dad had helped Laura and me to build a sort of den in the courtyard. We used an old tent, some of Dad's storage boxes, lots of cushions and an old sleeping bag with a broken zip. Mum hung an old white sheet over the top, so that you had to lift it up to climb inside. Laura and I ate our lunch in it and listened to stories. We were having a great time, but then Laura started bossing me about. 'Sit there.' 'Don't sit there.' 'I want the round cushion.' 'Go and get the Super-Secret book.' She kept ordering me about until we had a sort of row. I said, 'Stop telling me what to do, Bossy Boots.' She just sat up and folded her arms across her chest and said, 'Go if you don't like it.' So I got up, pulled open the white sheet and ran upstairs to our room. After a while I went into the bathroom to look out of the window. I could see her pretending to have fun in the den. I could hear her sort of chatting to herself but I knew Laura, and she wasn't very good at being on her own. It wasn't long before she came to find me.

ME: Sometimes, I would say I didn't want to do the things that she wanted to do, just so that . . . just so that . . .

AUNT SHELLY: Just so that she wasn't the one ordering you about?

I nodded.

AUNT SHELLY: I used to do that to your mum. I once pretended I really hated anything to do with ballet or dancing just because I knew she loved it. She was always telling me what to like and what not to like, especially after our dad died. Then she was double bossy!

I had never met Mum's dad – he died when she was at university – but I had seen lots of photographs of him.

ME: What was your dad like?

She pulled the duvet over her feet.

AUNT SHELLY: Very funny and kind. He loved reading, just like you.
ME: Were you very, very sad, you know, when he . . . ?

Aunt Shelly's voice got very quiet.

AUNT SHELLY: I was. It was very sad. But it gets better, you know. You always have a little sad feeling, like, if I see something that reminds me of him it can feel a little sad. But sometimes if I see a telly programme I know he would have loved or if I hear a bit of music he would have liked or a joke that would have made him giggle, I sort of laugh for him. I sort of laugh for the both of us.

I looked up to her and before I had a chance to think about it I said:

ME: Tonight I had dessert for the both of us.

Aunt Shelly laughed, held her hand out towards mine and squeezed it tightly.

So that night my mum's little sister fell fast asleep in Laura's bed, only she slept with her head where your feet are supposed to go and I discovered something else. I found out that even though Aunt Shelly is really, really pretty, and even though she has sort of princess hair that smells of lemons, I found out that she does have very, very stinky feet.

16

At breakfast Mum gave me a glass of juice. I looked down at the little white tablet and rolled it between my thumb and forefinger.

ME: Why do I have to take these again?

Mum looked over at Dad and they both sort of sighed.

MUM: Because . . .

I looked at Mum and at everyone else, they all looked weird.

AUNT SHELLY: To keep you fit and strong, young lady!

Then Rory suddenly flicked some jam across the table and it landed on Mum's blouse. Right on one of her boobs! We all laughed, all of us but Mum.

ME: Nice shot, Rory!

He did it again only this time the jam flew past my shoulder and landed on the wall behind me. Dad had to wrestle the jar from his tiny hands. For someone who's really little, Rory's super strong. If he grabs hold of something and you want it back, you better be prepared for a fight. Dad arm-wrestled with him for a bit, but Rory thought it was a game so he ran out into the hallway and lay down on the floor with the jar of jam underneath him. Then Rascoe jumped out of his basket and tried to get his nose into the jar.

Suddenly breakfast had turned into a giggling, barking, jammy mess so I swallowed the little white tablet and looked down at the back of the newspaper.

After breakfast we all said goodbye to Aunt Shelly and then Dad and I walked up the hill together to school. Today wasn't cold, it was that in-between weather. The sort of weather that makes you hot one minute and cold the next, as if it couldn't make up its mind. It was annoying and when it started spitting with rain Dad and I both sighed.

DAD: When is Spring going to get here?

I closed my eyes and remembered the weather report in the newspaper this morning.

ME: Not this week. This week it'll be cloudy with a chance of showers, a light to moderate south-westerly breeze. Yesterday was the coldest day in April since records began, but it was thirty degrees in Sydney and Auckland.

Dad laughed and kissed me goodbye.

*

After morning register, the door opened. Lexi walked into the classroom slowly and then she sat down at a different table on the far side of the room. The first lesson we had was English, and Miss Cauber spent ages talking to us about newspaper articles. We had to write our very own advert, but I couldn't think of anything I wanted to advertise. I sat there staring down at the blank page and then something odd happened. I was just about to write an advert for my favourite book when Lexi put her hand up.

MISS CAUBER: Yes, Lexi?

Everyone turned to look and her cheeks went rather pink.

LEXI: I . . . erm . . . could I? Will there? Is it?

A little sniggering began.

142

MISS CAUBER: Come on, Lexi, I haven't got all day.

LEXI: Sorry, I just forgot . . . I mean, I can't . . . what, er . . . which page are we supposed to be on?

And when Lexi turned around she held up her history text-book. The rest of the class laughed. Miss Cauber went over to Lexi and they chatted for what seemed like for ever. I could see Lexi's cheeks had turned from pink to bright red so I looked away. This time I decided that I would not stare or gawp or watch or do anything like that.

At lunch-break I went to get my book out of my bag and that's when I saw that I had forgotten to put the Super-Secret book back! It was still there at the bottom of my bag, sort of hiding inside another book. It must have been there since I went to Oxford. Why hadn't I put it back in my room? Just then Greta came barging into the classroom and I sort of jumped up and dropped it on the floor.

GRETA: Mr Fincher says you have to come outside now!

I bent down and tried to hide the special book behind my back.

GRETA: What's that?

ME: Nothing.

She folded her arms across her chest and sighed.

GRETA: You have to come outside. Like *everyone* else!

I put my Super-Secret book back inside my bag and pushed
the bag underneath my chair and started to follow Greta
outside. Then she turned around, leant in towards me,
sniffed, and in her horrid nasty voice she said,

GRETA: You smell a bit like a dog basket, you know. A
pizzary dog basket.

Then she laughed and ran outside. *Well*, I thought, *as long as
I don't smell like my aunt Shelly's feet, I don't care.*

I walked out to the playground and looked around to
see if I could see Lexi. I almost gave up and then I heard
her voice and caught sight of a flash of red hair. She was
playing football with all the boys. I walked across the
playground to get a better view. Not only was she playing
with them but she was *really good*. I watched her whizz
past Merrick and score a goal. Everyone on her team
cheered.

It made me think of Laura and then I heard something
very familiar. I heard a horrible whiney voice and it was
saying something that I knew very well and I felt my heart
beat faster. I turned around quickly and looked up towards
the picnic benches. *Greta!* She was sitting cross legged on top
of one of the picnic tables. Erin and Megan were sitting in
front of her and they were laughing. I tried to move, but it
was as though my legs wouldn't work.

Greta's voice got louder, my heart fluttered and my stomach kind of jumped up. In her horrid little hand was *my* Super-Secret book and she was reading it out for everyone to hear. I didn't run. Not at first. I didn't shout. Not straight away. Instead I took a deep, deep breath and screamed:

GIVE ME MY BOOK. GIVE ME MY BOOK NOW!

Everyone stopped moving and stayed absolutely still. It was as though we were all playing musical statues. Everyone froze, but Greta didn't stop reading and I could see her turning the pages without any care at all. She was going to rip it. She was going to ruin it!

Greta held up the book higher and I could see the pages being flapped around in the breeze. One of the purple feathers came away from the front cover and I watched it swirl around and slowly fall to the ground.

And all the time her voice just got louder and louder. I tried to move, but I couldn't and my heart beat quicker and quicker. I felt it flutter and flicker. *Thud, thud, thud.* Greta stood up and placed her hand on her hip. It was like the picnic table was her little stage and now she was reading one of my silly stories to the *entire school.* I shouted once more:

GIVE ME MY BOOK BACK NOW!

I don't know what I saw first. Was it the red hair or the yellow ball? It happened so quickly. Yes! It *was* the red hair.

That *is* what I saw first. I saw it whipping around Lexi's face as she ran and ran. Her right arm was turning at her side like a windmill. Just a flash of red hair and bright yellow ball heading towards the picnic table.

Greta turned slightly to the side but she didn't see Lexi running or the yellow ball as it flew out of her hand and zipped through the air.

I watched it.

Josh watched it.

Erin watched it.

Everyone watched it fly towards her.

Everyone saw it but Greta, so it must have been a shock when the hard yellow ball hit her straight on the side of her head. So hard that she toppled backwards and sort of sideways off the table.

My book dropped on to the table and Greta landed face first into the school vegetable garden. I ran over to the table and grabbed my book just as Greta was pulling herself up. She was covered in mud and had half a lettuce stuck to her shoe. She didn't look happy! I saw her try to wipe a bit of mud from her cheek. I watched as she tried to climb out of the slippery patch and when she lost her balance and sort of tumbled backwards again, everyone laughed.

LEXI: Not so great any more!

I looked around at the crowd that had gathered. I saw how they were all grinning and I suddenly realised that Greta had actually been mean and nasty to just about everyone at school. I just wanted to get away from horrible Greta and from everyone who had heard my silly stories, so I ran inside into the toilets. I sat down in a cubicle and tried to straighten out the pages of the book. It was a little crumpled and a few of the sequins had come off too but it was safe and I held it tightly to my chest. It was safe. *It was safe*.

I heard someone come into the toilets and then there was a loud knock on my cubicle door. I looked down and immediately recognised the shoes I could see in the gap below the door.

LEXI: Is it OK?

I unlocked the door and before I had a chance to say anything she had pushed her way in and locked the door behind her.

LEXI: Well?
ME: Thank you.
LEXI: It was good you know. The story I mean. Did you make that up?

I nodded.

ME: How did you do that? I mean it was kind of cool.
LEXI: I don't know. I guess I'm good at throwing and catching and running and stuff. Actually Dad always says

that, for someone like me, [she tapped the side of her head] I've got brilliant hand-eye co-ordination! It's good, you know, for sports and things.

Then she bent down to fasten one of her shoelaces. I watched her make one loop and then stop. Then she tried to make two loops, but they came undone. She tried again, folding one loop over the other, but that came undone too and she sort of sighed. It was like she couldn't get the laces to bend or as though her fingers wouldn't do what she wanted them to do. It was as if she hadn't ever had to do it before. I thought about my new school shoes and of how Laura would have hated the laces. I don't know why but this time it didn't make me cross. When I looked down at Lexi almost getting her fingers laced into knots just like Laura used to do it sort of made me smile.

LEXI: Oh! I hate these stupid shoes!

And then she looked up to me, a little bit like Rory does and so, for some reason, I put the Super-Secret book down, bent forward and I tied the laces for her. Her face was so close to mine that I could feel her breath upon my cheek. It was so close that I could see that she had hundreds of pretty freckles all over her face. It looked as though she had been flicked with a tiny brown paintbrush. Her eye, the one that I could see, wasn't blue at all. I had never seen a colour like it before. It was like the sea, like jewels, like my mum's favourite necklace. It was the most beautiful colour I had ever seen. It was sort of sparkly.

As Lexi tucked a strand of red hair behind her ear, I saw a little reddish scar below her eye patch. Then we heard a door open and the sound of grown-up shoes.

MISS CAUBER: Girls? What's going on?

She sounded really cross. Lexi and I stood up, unlocked the door and came out. Miss Cauber was standing by the sinks with her seriously angry face.

MISS CAUBER: Well, Lexi, I don't know what you were allowed to do at your last school, but at St Thomas we do *not* throw balls at other children. We do *not* come to class when we want. We do *not* stay in the toilets for as long as we like. We do not . . .

And suddenly Lexi burst into tears. Really loud, wailing, I've-just-fallen-over-and-broken-my-leg tears. Miss Cauber gasped.

MISS CAUBER: Oh, Lexi! I'm so sorry. I shouldn't have shouted. Emma, are you OK? You look very flushed.

Lexi made another loud sobbing noise so Miss Cauber bent down and put her arm around Lexi's shoulders.

MISS CAUBER: Would you like to go and get a glass of water?

Lexi was still crying, her head was tucked into Miss Cauber's side but as they left the toilets together, Lexi turned to me, smiled and with her one sparkly eye, she winked!

*

After school, the first thing I did was put the Super-Secret book back in its super-secret place. When I came back downstairs, Mum was unpacking the shopping and she asked me about my day. I didn't tell her about Lexi or what had happened with Greta, but when I saw her unpack a large pale green lettuce, I giggled.

MUM: So, are you hungry?

I was. I was starving. I was so hungry I felt like I could eat anything. I felt as though I could eat any of Mum's 'healthy and very good for you food' and I was just about to say exactly that when I sort of stopped myself and, seeing the bag of potatoes, I looked back up at her and grinned.

ME: Can I have some of your special mashed potatoes?

She looked at me strangely, as though I had asked for something really weird like beetroot and mustard or something, but then she kind of smiled.

That night Mum and Dad had a mini row about him

coming home late from work without telephoning, but I was so busy gobbling up the meal Mum had made that I wasn't really paying attention. I almost licked the plate clean. I was so tired that I forgot about the computer and I didn't mind one bit when Mum said I had to turn off the telly and go to bed.

<u>At bedtime</u>

VOICE: Greedy gobbler!

I laughed and rolled on my side, then I told Laura all about Greta, the Super-Secret book and how Lexi had come to *our* rescue.

*

On Sunday, Mum seemed to be in a really good mood so her and Dad took me and Rory into town. We didn't go up the hill to the village, but down the steep hill all the way to the river. I watched the sun peeking out from behind the tall block of apartments where I knew Greta had moved to after her parents got divorced. Dad stopped when he saw me looking up.

DAD: It's the one right at the top. Greta lives in The Penthouse.

I remembered all about the building. I had read about it in one of those grown-up magazines that come with the newspapers and without thinking I did it again.

ME: It's a Richard McAdams building which cost one hundred and twelve million pounds to build. Originally it was supposed to be an office block, but during the banking crisis of 2008 the investors sold the lease to The Wiley Brothers who turned part of the building into thirty-five luxurious apartments. The Penthouse has a state-of-the-art home cinema, parking for three cars, four bedrooms with ensuite marble bathrooms, under-floor heating, a sixty thousand pound hand-built kitchen, a home gym, a roof terrace with hot tub and three-hundred-and-sixty-degree views of the city.

Mum and Dad fell about laughing and Dad put his arm around my shoulders and kissed the top of my head.

DAD: Well, a home cinema sounds awesome.

Mum sighed and shook her head.

MUM: I don't know how important panoramic views are when you're ten years old, but I think Greta could do with more of a three-hundred-and-sixty-degree view of her mother.

I suddenly thought of how mean Greta was, of how she was always bragging about her mum being on the telly but I couldn't remember one time when I had seen Greta's mum pick her up from school. I had never seen her come to a school concert or chat with the other mums. It was always some kind of nanny or helper.

I was going to say something about what had happened at school but Rory suddenly broke free of Mum's hand and made a dash for the water, so we all ended up racing down the path together shouting, 'RORY! ROREEEE!'

After we ate the most delicious fish and chip lunch on an outside table, Dad announced that we could go to At-Bristol for a few hours too. It's one of my favourite places to go, because it's a sort of science centre place but it's not boring like normal museum places. You don't just stand and look at stuff in a glass box or anything like that, you actually DO the stuff in the box. You get to touch all the stuff and do experiments for real, like a proper scientist and somehow when you go home you kind of know lots of new stuff without really knowing how. Me and Laura used to love doing the experiment about gravity where you get to fly these parachute things high up into the air.

When we got home Mum said I could go on the computer and when I looked at my inbox there wasn't just one little yellow envelope, there were five! Five little yellow envelopes and they were all for me. Two were from Grandpa, but three of them were from Lexiland. I opened the first one, but there wasn't anything there, it was just an empty message. Then I clicked on the second one.

To: EddieE@hotmail.com
From: Lexiland@hotmail.com
Hi Eddie,
Sorry about that – I pressed the send key by mistake! I'm always doing that. Your email made me laugh. Here's a picture to make you laugh.
Lexi

I clicked on the little paper clip to open the attachment. It seemed to take forever, but when I saw the picture that Lexi had sent I laughed so loudly that it made Rascoe jump up out of his basket. It was a picture of a large mug with arms, legs and a head. But the head wasn't any old head, it was a photograph of Miss Cauber's head! On the front of the mug were the words, **My breath stinks and so does school!**

I opened the third email from Lexi.

To: EddieE@hotmail.com
From: Lexiland@hotmail.com
Eddie,
Well? Did you get it or what?
Lexi

So I replied.

I pressed send and printed off the mug picture because I knew exactly what I wanted to do with it. I was going to stick it in the Super-Secret book.

I ran upstairs to my bedroom and climbed on to the bedside cabinet so I could reach my secret hiding place. I knelt down on Laura's bed, opened up the book and turned the pages. But as I turned over the pages of colourful pictures, I suddenly felt a chill and my stomach did that weird flippy thing. Could I stick someone else's picture in *our* Super-Secret book?

I sat there for a while with the mug picture in one hand and the book in the other. I closed the book, looked down at the front of it and sighed.

The front cover had been another Laura creation. She had drawn both of our names in big silver and gold letters and stuck a photo of me above her name and a photo of her above my name. We knew the difference, but no one else would have. I traced my fingertip along her name, along the words *Secret* and *Keep out!* and I watched the tears drop on to the cover. When I turned it over to wipe it dry, I saw that there was nothing on the back cover. I flipped it open from the back and looked at the empty pages. Then I turned it upside down, cut around the picture and stuck it inside and in my best handwriting I wrote:

Monday April 12th
Lexiland

And then I stuck the picture in below.

At bedtime

VOICE: When you went to At-Bristol did you do the thing with the parachutes?

ME Yeah, Rory loved it.

VOICE: What about upstairs? Did you go upstairs?

ME: Oh it's changed now, Lor – they don't have that jungle walk thingy, they have this amazing animation stuff. You get to make your own cartoon and it was so funny because Rory and me made a sort of cat with two tails and . . .

But I stopped suddenly because Laura made a funny noise. I was just about to speak when I heard it again. At first I didn't know what it was. It was weird and when I did work out what it sounded like, I could feel something miserable too. It was like a really, really sad feeling but not like normal. It was like I wanted to cry, like I needed to cry *for* Laura.

I had got to see all the new stuff, but Laura didn't and I felt terrible again.

I rolled over and stared up at the luminous stars that Laura and I had stuck to the ceiling.

ME: What would you like for our new birthday?

Laura giggled once more.

VOICE: Five of everything, silly!

I laughed a bit too loudly. I heard someone come up stairs so I lay still and held my breath. There was a soft knock at the door.

MUM: Are you alright?

I tried not to laugh but the only way I could stop myself bursting into giggles was to keep holding my breath.

Mum opened the door, switched on the light and looked down at me quizzically and then really worriedly when I let out a huge gasp of air and breathed quickly again.

MUM: Are you absolutely sure there is nothing wrong? I mean, do you feel OK? We didn't overdo it today, did we? You sounded out of breath just now.

ME: There's nothing wrong . . . I am a bit thirsty actually.

Mum looked kind of worried and dashed off, coming back really quickly with a large glass of water. She watched me take a few sips.

MUM: If you do find that you feel a bit out of breath or something just tell me, won't you?

It seemed like a really weird thing to ask, but I nodded my head anyway and watched her leave. I decided that my mum is actually a bit strange.

VOICE: Were you really thirsty?

ME: Sort of.

VOICE: Now it's just you, you can have a mint-chocolate-chip ice-cream cake.

I thought about it for a second. I imagined a huge green and brown cake.

ME: Laura?

Silence.

ME: Laura . . . did you? Did you?

VOICE: Did I what?

ME: Did you? Did the cake? Did it make you? Laura . . . was . . . was it the cake's fault?

I held my breath. My heart beat quicker and quicker and fluttered and flickered. I rolled over and squashed my face into the pillow, but there was no sound. No sound apart from the *thud-thud thud-thud* of my heart and then I thought I heard a little sigh. A single, soft and silent sigh.

I think I heard a voice. I think I heard a something.

17

That night I had one long and horrible nightmare. It was so horrid and so scary that I woke up sort of shouting. Mum came into my bedroom to make sure I was OK and that I wasn't actually being chased by a giant spider who was trying to trap me and Laura underneath a massive coffee mug. Mum climbed into Laura's bed and promised to stay there until the morning, but when I woke up she wasn't there any more. She was gone and for some reason it made me feel really sad.

I climbed up on to my bedside cabinet to get the Super-Secret book. I needed to see Laura's drawings but when I tried to feel around I couldn't quite find it. I took one foot off the table and tried to reach further, but then I slipped off the table and fell into the book shelf.

I burst into tears. Really loud sobbing tears. Big, heaving,

wailing tears. Tears that make the snot run out of your nose.
Tears that make your head hurt. Tears that stop you from
being able to speak.

Dad came running in to see what had happened and
when he saw me in a crumpled heap on the floor he bent
down and put his arms around me, so I forced my sobbing,
snotty, teary face into the softness of his fleece.

DAD: What's the matter? Shhhh, there-there, come on,
calm down.

He rocked me back and forth a bit but all I could say was,
'Lorr-ra, Lorr-ra, Lorr-ra.'

When I'd calmed down, he told me that I could have the
day off school. He said that we could both stay at home and
have a Breakfast Bedroom Picnic for two.

I smiled and climbed back into bed. I could hear him
banging around in the kitchen for ages and as I waited for
my dad's version of toast to arrive, I felt better knowing that
today I could stay in my pyjamas. I didn't even mind the
burnt toast or the very, very hardboiled egg that Dad made
for me. After I had gobbled it down I felt a little sleepy, so I
lay back on the bed and closed my eyes.

When I woke up, Dad was on Laura's bed, his laptop was
next to him and he was talking on the phone so I lay still for
a while with my eyes shut.

DAD: Fiona, she is fine. Stop worrying. No, she hasn't been out of breath. No, I checked. She just needed a day off. I needed a day off. Fiona, you have got to stop worrying. You saw how she was on Sunday – running up and down the harbour-side with Rory with no problem at all. She's not ill. She just needs . . .

I waited for as long as I could. I wanted to hear what Mum and Dad were going on about but I couldn't keep the fart from coming out any longer and the loudest trombone-sounding fart echoed off the bedroom walls. Dad and I started laughing so much that he had to hang up the telephone.

DAD: Sleep OK?
ME: Better.
DAD: Glad to hear it. Do you want me to show you something fun?

I climbed out of my bed and on to Laura's.

DAD: Look. See that?

He pointed at a blue square on his laptop screen with the word *Messenger* at the top and in the corner was his name next to a green dot.

DAD: This is like email. But it's quicker. Instant.

He explained how I could tell whoever I wanted that I was there at my computer, and if they were at theirs then we could sort of chat.

DAD: Look, I'm online, and see that?

He pointed at the name J.O.E. I knew exactly who that was. That was Grandpa.

DAD: Well, he's logged in right now too.

I thought of Grandpa on his houseboat.

ME: Right now? Really?

I tried to imagine where Grandpa was; perhaps he was sitting at the little table.

DAD: You want to say hello?

So I typed:

EDDIE: Hi! I have to go to Grandma's house after school every day and she makes me do *stuff*! Where are you sitting?

I pressed enter and waited but it wasn't long before there was a *ping* sound and underneath my message was this:

162

J.O.E.: Hah! I'm sitting at the little table, but that sounds like your grandma. Well, I'm sure she's making you do lots of 'useful' things! It's really sunny here. Spring has arrived in Oxford at last!

We chatted for ages; it was great, like having Grandpa right there in the room with me. I told him all about Lexi and the funny picture, about Greta the Not-So-Great and how Dad let me stay at home because I had a really bad dream.

That night when Mum had finished giving Rory his bath, she came into the living room where Dad and I were watching the telly.

MUM: How are you feeling now, Emma? Dad says you and Grandpa were chatting online for ages.
ME: I'm fine, Mum, it was just a bad dream.

Mum looked down at me and sighed, but she and Dad kept looking at each other and every so often she looked up from the marking she was doing and sort of squinted at me over her glasses.

MUM: Emma, you know you said on Sunday that you were 'all out of breath'? Does that happen a lot?

My dad sat up and turned to Mum.

ME: You mean when I was chasing Rory?

Mum nodded.

ME: I just didn't want to, you know . . . play any more.
MUM: But did you feel like it was too hard running?
ME: Mum, it's always hard keeping up with Rory.

My dad sighed again. What was she going on about?

DAD: Fiona, come on. Let us watch the telly in peace, will you?

After that they started squabbling again and I started to think that maybe the only reason they argued was because of me. As I listened to their voices getting louder and louder, I started feeling bad. It was like I was making them row or something because most of the time the rows always started with something to do with me. I think I was about to cry, I think I was. I think I was about to shout at THEM. I felt like I was going to say something like STOP IT – in my new super-loud, scary voice – but I didn't because the telephone rang. It rang and rang until eventually Dad got up to answer it. I wasn't really paying attention until I heard him say, 'Eddie? Eddie? I think you have the wrong number.'

I sat up quickly and turned to look at him.

DAD: Sorry, what did you . . . Lexi?

I felt my heart beat a little quicker and I started nodding at Dad.

DAD: Oh! I'm sorry, I know who you are. Sorry, Lexi, Emma – I mean Eddie – has been telling me *and* her grandpa all about you.

My cheeks went all hot. For some reason I wished he hadn't said that last bit.

DAD: Of course you can, Lexi, just a minute.

Dad put his hand over the telephone and him and Mum made funny smiling faces at each other. Dad held out the phone and coughed.

DAD: Eddie . . . there is a Lexi Lister on the phone and she just *has* to talk to you.

I took the phone out of his hand and went quickly into the hall where Rascoe looked like he was having a funny dream too. I could hear Lexi's voice even before I put the phone to my ear and if I thought she talked pretty loudly and quickly before. I was wrong, because when she talked on the phone it was as though she didn't really need to breathe at all. It was as though she was shouting all the way from wherever it was that she lived. She had so many questions, but every time I went to answer one of them, she sort of answered for me.

LEXI: So were you ill today?

ME: Well, I . . .

LEXI: I sometimes get to stay off school even if I am not really poorly. Like one time my mum wanted us to visit her best friend, Jane and her son Zack, which was so cool because Zack has the cutest dog you ever saw, but they live in London so I missed three days of school, remember? Oh, and one time Dad was coming back from being in New York and we went to pick him up from . . . you know . . . er . . . you know, Eddie, the . . .

ME: Train station?

LEXI: No . . . the . . .

ME: Airport?

LEXI: That's it! We had to go get him and it's like a really, really long way from here and so I got to stay off school – remember? Anyway, I'm not in school for the rest of the week because I've got to go to Oxford for a thingy at the Greenview place. Oh, but I can text – what's your mobile number?

Oxford? Greenview place? Mobile number? My head was spinning. I didn't have a mobile. I knew Greta had her own mobile, but I didn't. My dad was always losing his and my mum's nearly always ran out of battery.

166

ME: I don't . . . er, have . . .

LEXI: You don't have a mobile? Like, really? Weird! Oh I know! Messenger – you know?

And this time I did know what she was talking about so before Lexi said she had to go, we agreed that we would try to do the Messenger thing too, just like I had done with Grandpa.

That night I went to bed a little bit excited. I wanted to tell Laura all about my phone conversation with Lexi, but I think I fell asleep as soon as I closed my eyes.

*

The next few days at school were sort of OK actually, just the same old school stuff. But I did notice one thing that was a bit strange on Thursday lunchtime. Greta the Not-So-Great was sitting all by herself on one of the benches looking really miserable and I hadn't ever seen that before.

After school I didn't need to go to Grandma's house – Mum and Rory met me at the school gates and in her hand was a paper bag I recognised immediately. *Bateman's Bakery*. My dad's favourite. She handed me the stripy blue bag and I knew exactly what would be inside. I pulled the sticky iced bun out of the bag but before I took a bite, I noticed Rory looking up at me. His eyes were all red and puffy and his thumb was stuck in his mouth.

MUM: Rory has had a bit of a bad day, haven't you, boo?

Rory sort of hiccupped and nodded at the same time.

MUM: Rory learnt something new today, didn't you, Rory?

He nodded again. I could see that he was trying to stop himself from crying. He kept gulping and biting on his bottom lip but snotty tears were running down his face.

MUM: Rory has just found out what happens if you want all of the Lego all of the time.

Rory snivelled.

RORY: Must-let-go-lego.

I watched him wipe his nose on the sleeve of his little coat.

RORY: Got-to-sh-sh-share.
MUM: That's right, boo, you can't have all the toys on you own, can you? What about the other little ones?

Rory nodded his head.

RORY: Got-to-do-shar-ring now. Ror-ree *will* be a g-g-g-good boy he will.

And with that he started to sob. I looked down at little Rory.

168

Poor Rory. I used to get told off for the exact same thing. I remember being told that I wouldn't have any friends if I didn't learn how to share but I hadn't needed other friends. I hadn't needed anyone else. I had Laura and even though she was super bossy, she was really good at sharing. Sometimes if I ate up all of my crisps first or if I gobbled up my sweets too quickly, she would always give me her last one, even if it was her favourite. Suddenly I didn't feel like eating the iced bun any more, but when I told Mum, she started fussing again and said that maybe we were walking home a bit too quickly. She even made us have a little rest on the bench in the Square.

When we got home I was feeling a bit miserable and when Dad came home and saw my gloomy face he got his laptop out and said I could chat to Grandpa if I wanted to, but I had an even better idea.

It didn't take long before I heard a little *ping* and even though I was sitting on the sofa next to Dad and Lexi was out at some place called Greenview, it was just like we were right next to each other. And she had lots to say. She had tons of things to tell me.

1. Hannah is her mum.
2. Her dad is from America, but Hannah was born in Bristol.
3. Hannah used to be a famous dancer but she hurt her foot so now she just has a kind of hobby and looks after Lexi.
4. Her dad is nearly always working and she doesn't get to

see him much.

5. The boy she was emailing on the last day of term was Ethan, who's her cousin and lives in San Francisco where her dad is from and that also has a gigantic bridge.

6. Lexi hates Greta (or almost hates her).

7. Greenview is a kind of hospital and she was there today with her Mum having a check-up which didn't hurt or anything.

8. She has her own laptop and was sitting in bed.

9. She doesn't have any pets, but her mum has promised her a kitten for her birthday.

10. She was born in New York, but she doesn't remember anything about it because she was a titchy baby when they moved to England.

11. Even though she'd cried, Mrs McWatter and Miss Cauber had really told her off about the Yellow Ball Incident and Hannah was really cross too.

12. She lives at number 14 Canning Circus.

I showed Dad the screen. His eyes widened and he sort of whistled.

DAD: Wow. Your new friend lives in one of the biggest, most beautiful houses in all of Bristol.

Dad explained where Canning Circus was and it was really, really close. It was just on the other side of the park. It was right by the zoo.

Then there was another *ping*.

Lexiland: Do you wanna come over after school on Friday? We are driving back then so we can meet you outside Kaycees.

Did I want to? Another 'no brainer'! So it was arranged. I was so excited that I could feel my heart beating really quickly, but when I told mum that my heart was fluttering just like when you get butterflies in your stomach she wasn't very happy. She got all serious and strange and asked me lots of weird questions and even bent down and put her head to my chest. Dad got really angry with her and told her to stop being 'overprotective' and to stop upsetting me. I didn't understand what they were arguing about.

In the end I decided that maybe my mum is frightened of everything: bikes, cakes, running and now the sound of my heartbeat.

*

That night as I lay in my bed, I tried to imagine what Lexi's house would look like. Would it really be like the houses we saw in Oxford?

I was just drifting off to sleep when I saw the door open and close, and as I couldn't see anyone, I knew exactly who it was.

ME: Go back to bed, Rory!

171

But by the time I switched on the snow globe his little face was about an inch from mine. He was wearing his blue bear pyjamas. They used to be mine. Laura had a pair too, but hers were yellow. Why did I have a stupid little brother now and not Laura?

ME: Go back to bed and take your silly *wurple* rabbit with you.

Rory walked back towards the door and as I turned off the snow globe he kind of looked back at me over his shoulder. Then I heard another sigh.

VOICE: He wants a cuddle, you idiot!
ME: Laura?
VOICE: He wants a cuddle.

There was a silence and at first I wondered if Rory had heard the voice too but he didn't say anything and I *knew* he was still there. I rolled over on to my back and sighed. I thought about his sad little face. I remembered his tears on the way back from school and I thought that when I had been Rory's age at least I had Laura to play with. I had Laura to share with.

ME: Rory?

There was a little snivel.

RORY: Hmmm.

ME: You wanna cuddle?

I heard the patter of his feet and the next thing I knew he had climbed up on to the bed and under the covers. I felt a rabbit ear go up my nose and then I remembered the song my Mum used to sing to me and Laura.

ME: *Can I be your cuddle pot? Will you be my cuddle pie?*

He giggled and it wasn't long before he fell fast asleep and started doing his little piglet snoring. For some reason, I thought it was kind of cute. I mean, he can be the most annoying little boy that you've ever met, and sometimes when Mum spoils and fusses over him or when he does the Rory Roar all weekend I really do wish that I still had my sister instead. But, as I listened to his little Wilbur-like snorts, I kind of felt bad.

I felt one of his little hands curl into mine and I felt bad that I'd ever wished him away. He wasn't Laura but he was kind of, maybe, possibly, sort of, a little bit sweet. He wasn't Laura but he was my little one.

I heard a faint sigh.

VOICE: That's better.

18

On Friday morning I waved goodbye to Mum and Rory, ran into school and for the first time in ages I didn't mind being there at all. I didn't mind that we spent the entire morning doing drama, which I hate. I didn't mind that I had to sit by Merrick at lunchtime. I didn't mind about the horrid swimming lessons where I had to swim up and down the pool whilst being kicked and splashed in the face. I didn't mind at all that my eyes stung and my wet hair dripped down my back so that my jumper sort of stuck to me all the way back to school. I didn't mind at all.

I couldn't wait for the end of the day, and when the final bell rang, I didn't walk out of school – I ran. I didn't walk through the Square – I ran. I almost bumped into the stinky pigeon man. I didn't watch out for cars and buses or walk carefully through the village like I'm supposed to.

I hurried past Reg the Veg and the cake shop and by the time I got to the door of Kaycees I was out of breath and my face was all hot and sweaty. But I didn't care. I didn't care at all.

And then I waited.

After a while I decided to take my rucksack off because the strap was kind of pinching.

Then I waited, and waited some more.

My legs started to ache a bit so I sat down on the little bench where I had seen Lexi with her strawberry laces. My feet didn't quite reach the ground so I just sort of swung my legs back and forth for bit.

Then I heard my name being called, but when I turned to look it was just one of my mum's friends so I waved hello and I looked down at my watch. I'd been waiting for half an hour.

I stood up and looked down the street. I felt my stomach flip over and my heart beat faster and faster. *She's not coming,* I thought. *She's not coming.* It had all just been some kind of joke. My chest felt tight and heavy and tears ran down my cheeks.

I put my rucksack back on and started to walk back towards my house. I felt sort of heavy, like I had a bag of sand upon my head. I was just turning into the road beside the bridge when I heard someone shouting behind me. At first I thought it was an angry driver shouting, '*Ready, ready, ready,*' but then I turned around. Running across the green towards me were Hannah and Lexi. *They had come!* They hadn't forgotten! It hadn't been a joke!

Seeing them running towards me with their crazy red hair flying around their faces, and hearing them shout my name made me smile my biggest ever smile. It was a smile that came all the way from my tummy right up to my face. I had a feeling that made me grin, giggle and feel a bit tingly all at the same time. When they reached me, *they* had sweaty red faces and *they* were both panting and sort of gasping for breath.

HANNAH: Eddie, Eddie, I am so, so, so sorry. We were on our way back from Oxford and my car broke down. I couldn't get hold of the school in time and then we had to wait for the AA to come and fix it and they couldn't fix it so they drove us all the way back home and I thought it was quarter past two, but it was quarter past three and so we just had to run. We just had to leg it, didn't we, Lexi?

Lexi had sort of bent over and was trying to catch her breath.

LEXI: Eddie . . . car . . . old . . . stupid . . . ran . . . here . . .
HANNAH: You must have been worried. I hope you didn't think we'd forgotten. You'll still come, won't you? Lexi's being talking about it all day, haven't you?

Lexi blushed and straightened up her patch but I didn't hear what she said after that because Hannah started talking again and she talked as quickly and as loudly as Lexi did.

We walked back over the green, past The Merchants Houses, past the turning to school and along a wide tree-lined road all the way up towards the zoo. For a minute I thought that was where we were going but, just before the entrance to the zoo, we turned left down a narrow passageway. I had been to the zoo a lot, with Laura, Mum, Dad, Rory, and the school even brought us here once. When I went with the school we had to listen to a funny little man talk about the rainforest. All I remember was he had looked just like Mr Potato Head. He didn't have one single hair on his head, but when he came to stand closer to me, I noticed that he had lots of hair coming out of his ears and nose. I'd been to the zoo a lot but I'd never noticed the little passageway before. It was very narrow and on each side there were high red brick walls. I noticed bits of graffiti and old posters for concerts and when I told Hannah that I hadn't ever seen the passage before, she said that you could walk past it every day and not even know that it was there.

Then we turned down some metal steps and Hannah's red clogs made a really loud *clackety-clack* noise all the way down. When finally we reached Canning Circus it was unlike anything I had seen before. It wasn't a straight road with houses on both sides; it wasn't a super-steep road with titchy houses and a noisy railway line, like my road. It was sort of circular. The houses were even bigger than the ones I'd seen in Oxford. They were taller, wider, prettier and each one was a yellowy colour, a bit like sand. I turned around and around and saw that the houses were in a sort of circle or two semi-circles. In the very middle was a garden but it wasn't like the square garden that I'd seen inside the old building in Oxford. It wasn't neat and green and tidy. It was surrounded by lots of different trees and all around the sides were black metal railings, a bit like a park. I saw a gate with the sign *Canning Circus Gardens – Private*, but you couldn't really see much more because of all the trees. There were three copper beeches, an oak, a silver birch and my favourite was the horse chestnut. It was enormous with long curving branches that created a sort of archway across the road. I reached up with one hand to touch its white conical flowers and the only sounds were bird song and the faint rush of the breeze. I stood for a moment and smelt the air; it was perfumed and sweet. No beeping horns and dirty fumes. No clattering trains and roaring engines. I closed my eyes and then I heard a very loud, very real, very scary roar. And it wasn't Rory. The roar roared again and I jumped. Lexi giggled.

LEXI: I didn't believe them when they said the new house was so close to the zoo that you can hear the roaring lions. I thought they were just teasing me, but the day after we moved in I heard it three times. You

kind of get used it. I guess they're hungry or something.

There was another roar, but this time we both laughed. I
followed Lexi through a little gate towards the house. The
front door was painted shiny black with the number four-
teen in golden brass and it had a door knocker in the shape
of a tiny lion's face. Hannah had to search through her bag
for the keys so I turned around and looked back at the
garden. Even from here you couldn't really see it; it was
private, it was hidden, it was sort of secret. Lexi leant towards
me and whispered in my ear.

LEXI: That's just for us. You can only go in it if you live
here. You have to have the key.

Eventually Hannah found her keys, opened the shiny black
door and they both stepped inside, but I didn't. I stayed still
and stared. It was like I was stuck to the step or something.
At the far end of the hall was a large window. Sunlight shone
brightly towards me; it lit up the floor, it lit up the pale
yellow walls and reflected off a large mirror into my eyes. On
the right-hand side of the hall was a staircase that curved
around to the left, and along the other side was a large table
with lots of silver photograph frames. Hanging down from
the ceiling was special kind of light, like the ones you see in
palaces or churches. It had three tiers of glistening glass
which sparkled and dazzled like an enormous crown.

179

LEXI: Come on, Eddie! Shoes off!

Eddie, I thought. *Eddie*. I loved being called Eddie and as I turned the name over and over in my head, I decided there and then that I would always like to be called that. I watched Lexi kick off her shoes – they flew across the black-and-white tiles and I realised that the floor was almost just like a chequer board. I looked up and saw that she was already halfway up the stairs but I didn't move. My feet *wouldn't* budge. I looked up towards Lexi. For a moment she seemed to frown, then she put her hands on the banister, lifted herself up, slid all the way down and landed perfectly in the middle of the chequered floor. She spun around to face me.

LEXI: What's up?

I said nothing so she turned to the mirror and adjusted her eye patch.

LEXI: Stupid thing itches.

I waited.

LEXI: I'm getting a new one next week.

For a minute I thought she was going to take it off, but then she looked back at me, smiled and held out a freckly hand.

So I reached out and took it. Suddenly I felt much braver, and I stepped in through the shiny black door, on to the chequer board tiles and into Lexiland.

19

Lexiland was enormous! It had five bedrooms, three bathrooms, a drawing room, a laundry room, a playroom, a music room, a cellar, a garden room *and* a kitchen that was big enough for a long wooden table and two sofas. There were four flights of stairs and one of those went all the way up to the roof where there was another garden that Lexi called the 'roof terrace'. Lexi gave me a tour and unlike when I walked her around the school, this time it really was a 'grand tour'.

LEXI: This is the drawing room.

ME: For drawing?

LEXI: No, silly, for sitting and stuff. For hanging out but we nearly always stay in the kitchen.

I looked around at the drawing room. Two large windows reached from almost the floor right up to the ceiling and you could just about see into the hidden garden in the circle outside. There was a huge fireplace and three sofas that were sort of arranged in a funny way. Two faced each other and the big red one faced the fireplace. None of them was in front of a telly like they normally are. In between the sofas there was a large wooden table with piles of neatly stacked magazines and a silver vase filled with a type of flower that I'd never seen before.

I looked up at the walls which were covered in paintings. One picture was larger than our school white-board, one had lots of multi-coloured paint splatters and there was a really pretty one of a boat out at sea which made me think of the front cover of *Tom Flemming and The Painted Sea*. Above the fireplace were lots of photographs and candlesticks and I could see that the wax had dripped down the side and was sort of hanging above the carpet like a waxy icicle.

Lexi went over to one side of the room and opened a door. It wasn't a normal door, it folded and folded apart until there wasn't really much wall left and I could see into the room next door.

Lexi said that that room was the music room. In the middle of the room, underneath another one of the special lights that I'd seen downstairs, was a large black piano. It wasn't anything like Grandma's tiny piano, it was huge. It was like the pianos you see on the telly, or at big concerts like the one I'd been to with Laura and Dad a few years ago.

It was beautiful. I ran up to it and stroked my hand down its silky sides. I walked around it and around it and sighed. For some reason I really wanted to lift up the lid and play something, anything, and I'd never felt like that before. At Grandma's, piano practice always seems like hard work, but I just knew that playing a beautiful piano like Lexi's would be magical!

ME: It's . . . very . . .

LEXI: I used to have these really boring lessons and I'd moan about them all the time. One day at my old house I was sitting at that stool not really wanting to practise and Dad just closed the lid and told me that I should only play it if I really wanted to and I told him I hated it. I told him I hated it more than mint chocolate-chip ice cream, the dentist and maths all put together. You know, nothing that tastes like toothpaste should ever taste like chocolate too. Don't you think?

That made me feel funny. It made me think of Laura, like she was standing right next to me. It was a different sort of funny feeling, not bad or weird or sad. It made me feel something good but I don't know what to call it yet.

LEXI: Dad hates anyone touching his 'special piano'. Once he shouted at my mum's friend for putting a drink down on it, look!

I bent over the lid and saw a faint ring mark on the top. We had lots of those ring marks on our kitchen table.

LEXI: He was really upset about that.

I looked up at the walls and noticed that there were lots of posters that I recognised but I couldn't think why. Lexi saw me looking at them.

LEXI: Those are my dad's shows.

In the far corner of the room was a little desk and above it was another huge poster inside a frame. A poster that I knew. There was a large moon and three stars and the words *The Moon, The Stars and the King of Omar*. It was a musical that I had been to see with Mum, Laura and Grandma. It had been during the Christmas holidays and the four of us had got the train all the way to London to see it. It was amazing and Laura and I had sung one of the songs all the way back home.

LEXI: My dad did the music, you know, that's what he does. He makes up music for shows and things.

I looked at all of the posters again and I realised that I knew nearly every one.

ME: Wow! I saw that one.

I pointed to the one above the little desk.

LEXI: I Love that one.
ME: I saw it with Laura, one Christmas.

When I turned back to Lexi she looked really sad.

LEXI: I hate Christmas!

I waited for her to tell me why but then she grabbed my hand and we went up to her room instead.

Being at Lexiland was great! She showed me lots of new things like:

1) How to slide all the way down the banister without falling off.
2) How to eat spaghetti with a knife and fork.
3) How to make funny pictures on the computer.
4) And how to paint your fingernails with three different colours. (I went home with yellow, pink and orange fingernails.)

It was the best time I'd had in ages but it went so fast that when Mum came to pick me up, me and Lexi begged for ten minutes more. I watched Hannah and Mum disappear into the kitchen and we just ran as fast as we could back upstairs.

Later, I climbed into bed and pulled the covers up to my chin. *Lexiland*, I thought. *Lexiland*. It was almost magical. I was just thinking if Mum would let me buy some of the multicoloured nail polish with my pocket money when Dad popped his head around the door.

DAD: What did you get up to at Lexi's house?

I lay back on my bed and grinned.

DAD: You had a good time then?
ME: Lexi's dad makes up music for . . .
DAD: I know, he's Max Lister. *The* Max Lister. They call him Max Maestro. He's a genius, you know.

Then he laughed and told me to turn out the light. I really wanted to tell Laura all about it too, but I was so tired that I fell asleep really quickly.

<u>At breakfast</u>
MUM: Eddie.

I looked up at her and smiled.

MUM: Hannah and I were talking last night and she and Lexi want to know if you'd like to go to their house next Friday too, unless you'd rather go to Grandma's.

I didn't need to answer, I just grinned at her.

*

The next week of school wasn't the same as it usually was. It was kind of easy and almost fun. Lexi met me at the corner every day and we walked into school together. On Wednesday she asked Miss Cauber if she could move tables. I don't know what Lexi said to her but it seemed to work because when we came back from lunch-break, Lexi was sitting in the chair right next to me and from then on we were always together at school.

I didn't just go to Lexiland that Friday, I went every Friday for three weeks. It was great! Lexi and I had lots of fun and she told me everything about herself, but she never said why she had to wear an eye patch and I decided that Aunt Shelly was right – I shouldn't ever ask.

The third Friday my mum came to pick me up from Canning Circus, she brought Rory with her. He didn't get stuck to the front step like I had done. Instead he ran straight up to Lexi, pointed, and said in a very loud voice, 'Look! Pirate!' At first no one said anything. Then Lexi bent down to Rory and in her bestest pirate voice she said, 'Arghhh! Come on, Little Rory. I know the way. Let's find the treasure. Anchors away!'

Everyone laughed and from that moment on Rory was a bit in love with my new best friend.

Lexi let him sit on her lap while Mum and Hannah chatted. She let him climb all over her and pull her red curls. She went into the playroom, came back with a book and by the time we had to leave she had read it four times and Rory was curled up beside her with his thumb in his mouth and his head on her shoulder. Lexi carried him to the front door and, as Mum prised him off her, he pointed at the patch again.

I almost shouted at him for that, but he just wrinkled his nose took his thumb out of his mouth and said, 'Why you got that?'

I gasped and held my breath but Lexi bent down to face him and whispered something in his ear. Rory's eyes widened and before he stepped out of the house he turned back to Lexi and smiled.

RORY: You losted it? Well, I will go and look for it then.

Hannah, Lexi and my mum burst out laughing, but I didn't really understand what was so funny.

*

Sunday was my mum's birthday. She wasn't too happy about it, even though Dad bought her a beautiful heart-shaped necklace. She said if I could change my birthday date, she could change her date of birth so, she was thirty-nine again. Which seemed really silly to me – why would anyone want to be younger?

That night I had a phone call from Lexi.

LEXI: Hannah says that you can stay the night on Friday, if your mum says it's OK.

ME: I'll have to ask. But she might say no.

LEXI: Well ask her! Unless you don't want to stay?

So before I went to bed I asked Mum but she just did lots of sighing and head scratching. She looked over at Dad. He sort of shrugged.

MUM: Maybe another time, eh?

DAD: Fiona, come on. It's just a sleepover.

And so it went on and on and on. I didn't know who was going to win but I had my fingers crossed that it would be Dad. At one point Mum told me to go upstairs and get ready for bed so I left the room but as I shut the door I heard my dad speak in a kind of pleading voice.

DAD: Fiona, you've met Hannah. There's nothing to worry about. She's made a new friend. It's helping her to have someone to hang out with. Perhaps we need to start helping each other.

Then Mum said something really quietly that I couldn't hear.

DAD: Fiona, it's not fair. We have to try to move on, we can't stay stuck with Laura at the back of the wardrobe!

Stuck at the back of the wardrobe? Laura was stuck at the back of the wardrobe? I felt my whole body stiffen and the sound of my heartbeat throbbed into my ears. Every hair on my body seemed to stand up so that it felt as though I was being pricked all over by lots of tiny needles and the floor seemed to tip underneath my feet a bit like it did on Grandpa's houseboat. I don't remember cleaning my teeth or washing my face. I don't remember changing into my pyjamas or climbing into bed. I forgot about my Super-Secret book, about Lexi and the sleepover. I lay there still and silent. I turned off the snow globe and waited.

I turned on my side and even though it was dark I could just make out the window and the side of Laura's bed.

ME: Laura, was Dad telling the truth? Are you stuck at the back of the wardrobe?
VOICE: Yeah and it's a bit smelly too. Dad keeps leaving his stinky trainers in here.
ME: Laura?
VOICE: Did you know that Mum has six pairs of black trousers and they are all exactly the same? She even has two pairs of boots which still have the price tag on and a really funny dress that looks like a Christmas tree decoration.

I knew exactly which dress she meant and it really did look just like a Christmas tree decoration. Mum wore it to a party when Rory had just learnt to walk and when he saw Mum in the silly dress he had sort of screamed and run away. I remember everyone laughing about it for ages. Dad said the dress was so bad it was scary, but Mum didn't mind. She always used to wear clothes that were a bit crazy. Now she seems to wear the same boring clothes that look a bit like a school uniform.

I heard a knock at the door and Mum came in to say goodnight. She stood at the door for ages and after a while she sat down on the end of Laura's bed. I turned my back to her and said nothing.

MUM: I really liked the birthday card you made me.

I said nothing.

MUM: I really . . .

I waited.

MUM: I wanted to . . .

I waited.

MUM: I hope you have good dreams tonight.

And then she sighed a bit and tucked my duvet around my toes.

MUM: Night, night.

I said nothing, waited for her to leave, rolled over on to my back, squeezed my eyes shut and held my breath again.

VOICE: That was rude of you.
ME: Are you really stuck at the back of the wardrobe?
VOICE: Sort of.

20

I used to think that you could have either good dreams or bad dreams. I used to think that you could only have nightmares that scared you or dreams that made you feel happy. But I have decided that you can have more than two kinds of dream. There are some that make you feel sad, like when you wake up thinking its Christmas Day only to find out it's just another ordinary Monday. My dad calls them 'disappointing dreams', and I have them a lot. I wake up and think that everything is the same. I forget. For a tiny moment I think Laura will be lying in the bed next to mine. Then I wake up, turn over, see the empty bed and I remember. I remember and I feel disappointed and miserable all over again. Sometimes, I think that if I lie there long enough, if I close my eyes for long enough, if I wish hard enough, Laura really will come back. If I go to sleep chatting to her I can get such a shock when the morning comes and I see that she's not there.

Those are the times when I feel so sad I can't even cry. Those are the times I can get really cross with Laura. Those are the times when I feel really angry, so angry that when I come down for breakfast I want to kick Rory's stupid train set across the room. But now I knew. Now I knew what Grandma had meant. Now I knew the truth: Laura was at the back of the wardrobe and I was going to get her out.

At breakfast

MUM: I've spoken to Hannah and she says Lexi would love to have a sleepover here on Friday instead. What do you think?

I grunted at her. I wasn't going to tell her that I thought that sounded great because I was still really cross about the way she'd acted the night before. Then I had an idea. I thought about the wardrobe and I realised that it would be better if Lexi came here. It would be much better because I had a plan. Dad got up from the table and put on his coat.

DAD: Fiona, that's not going to change anything, is it?

Mum sighed and put the cereal box back in the cupboard. It looked as though she was thinking of something to say but Dad left the house before she had a chance to speak.

I watched Mum tidy away the rest of the breakfast stuff and after she had finished wiping up after Rory, who had managed to get his jammy fingers on nearly every single chair, she sat down opposite me but sort of turned to the side. Then she didn't move at all, but just sat staring silently and when Rory came running back into the room she didn't even look up. He stopped flying his tractor above his head and stood still. He looked at her, then at me and then he walked over to her and tried to find what she was looking at.

RORY: What you doing, Mummy?

Mum sort of sat up quickly as though she had forgotten where she was.

MUM: Oh! Er, nothing. Sorry, sweetheart!

Rory set down his little tractor, climbed up on to the seat next to her and folded his tidgy arms across his chest.

RORY: I will do nothing much too!

Mum and I laughed and I finished off my toast, swallowed the little white tablet and headed for school because I had to meet Lexi before class. I needed her help.

I waited at the corner for a while but as it got later and later I decided that it must be one of those mornings where Lexi had overslept again.

I was right. Hannah brought her into school after morning registration so I didn't get a chance to talk to her. We had to do more stupid poetry that morning, but Lexi is really good at that. She's brilliant at finding lots of different rhyming words so it wasn't long before we had our very own poem. It was really funny, but Miss Cauber didn't think so – she kept having to tell us to stop talking and giggling. After break she got so fed up with the two of us that she suddenly stopped talking in the middle of a sentence.

Everyone stopped working and looked up.

MISS CAUBER: Sorry to interrupt Lexi and Emma's conversation, but do you think that you could stop talking please and get through the rest of this maths lesson quietly?

We both nodded and tried really hard to be quiet, but Lexi wasn't doing the maths exercise like she was supposed to. Instead she was creating a little cartoon at the back of her maths book. She was using the little squares to make bigger boxes and each one had a sort of funny face and a speech bubble inside. It was like a comic. Before we knew what was happening, Miss Cauber was standing right behind us. She leant over and took the book out of Lexi's hands.

MISS CAUBER: Interesting, Lexi, I have coffee breath, do I?

Everyone laughed.

MISS CAUBER: And Mr Fincher is a . . .

Everyone laughed again.

MISS CAUBER: I think perhaps you two need some time apart. Lexi, pick up your stuff and go and work by the art corner.

I watched Lexi slowly walk over to the far corner of the classroom where she had to sit down with her back to everyone. Miss Cauber bent down to my right ear and spoke in a quiet voice.

MISS CAUBER: Just because you can do maths with your eyes shut doesn't mean that it is fair for you to distract someone who can't.

Greta sort of stared at me and smiled her nasty smile. I felt myself get angry. Why was I getting told off for being good at maths? It wasn't fair! So I sort of frowned, stared and sighed at the same time.

Poor Lexi had to stay in at breaktime and lunchtime. She had to do all the maths work that I'd let her copy out of my book and she was really grumpy about it.

She was grumpy and moody with me the next day too so I didn't have any chance to talk to her about staying over on Friday, or about my Laura plan.

*

On Wednesday morning I was sitting at the breakfast table, thinking about my new birthday. It was already June, but I still didn't know what to ask for. Lexi wanted a kitten for her birthday and she seemed to think that getting a kitten was the bestest thing in the world, but I still couldn't think of anything I really had to have. Every time I started to think about it, I realised I couldn't think of anything I wanted more than . . . more than . . . more than having Laura back.

DAD: Earth to Eddie?

I grinned. I know it's a sort of boy's name, but I really loved my new name. I don't know why but it felt sort of special to have a name that no one else had and some of the girls and boys from my class had started to call me Eddie too. Before I was just 'the other twin' or 'Laura's sister'. Now I was Eddie.

When I arrived at school, Lexi and Hannah were waiting for me at the corner. As I got closer, I could tell they were having a bit of an argument.

HANNAH: You *will* apologise. You will apologise *today* and I don't want to hear anything more about it. We've talked about this and you can't have it both ways. You can't come crying to me when someone upsets you if you are going to be mean to someone else.

LEXI: But she is always picking on me!

HANNAH: I find that very hard to believe. Eddie?

I looked up and realised she was asking me. She wanted me to pick sides.

ME: Do you mean Greta?

HANNAH: No. I mean Miss Cauber. Never mind, Eddie, go on, off you go, or you'll be late again.

We waved goodbye, Lexi grabbed me by the arm and we both headed off through the Square.

LEXI: Thanks for sticking up for me! I've got to write an apology to Miss Cauber. I have to take it to her and say sorry too. I have to do all six exercises from that horrid purple maths book and if I don't do it I can't come to yours on Friday.

The purple maths book was for year threes, not for us. It was much bigger than the one I used. You had to do things like count with pretend money or colour in half of the apples or a quarter of a bar of chocolate. It was really easy but it wasn't for our class.

ME: But the purple book is for babies.

200

As soon as the words came out of my stupid, idiotic mouth, I knew it was the wrong thing to have said. I felt my cheeks go red, but Lexi looked as though I'd slapped her across the face. She ran off into school without me and didn't speak to me for the rest of the morning. I tried to find her at lunchtime but it seemed as though she had disappeared. I looked in the library, the computer suite and I even checked the toilets. When I wandered back outside I found Josh and Merrick sitting by the sports hut.

ME: Have you seen Lexi?

Josh shook his head and carried on searching for treasure up his left nostril and Merrick just lifted his bottom up and, by way of answering, he farted.

When Miss Cauber took the afternoon register she pointed at Lexi and asked her to stand up.

MISS CAUBER: Don't you have something for me, Lexi?

Lexi frowned and looked down at the floor. A strand of curly red hair hung down over her face.

MISS CAUBER: Lexi? I'm waiting.

I saw Lexi's freckly hands clench the back of the chair. Miss Cauber let out a sigh.

MISS CAUBER: Have you at least finished some of the maths work?

There wasn't a sound. Everyone waited but Lexi just kept on staring at her shoes.

MISS CAUBER: OK. Off you go then. Mrs McWatter would like a word with you.

There was a gasp from the entire class, and as Lexi left the room I saw a tear run down her right cheek. It made me feel horrid, like it was all my fault and then I realised that it was. Lexi's tears *were* my fault or at least I was partly to blame. If I'd only kept my mouth shut in class yesterday or helped her with Hannah this morning or not said the stupid thing about the purple book. What if she didn't want to be friends with me any more?

After school, Grandma was waiting at the school gates and she was in a rush. I looked back into school and could just about see the back of Lexi and Hannah's heads as they went into Mrs McWatter's office.

Grandma had lots of things to do, as usual. So I helped her in the garden, in the vegetable patch, in the kitchen and I even did my piano practice without grumbling. She said she was 'very impressed', but I didn't feel any better. When I got home I went on the computer and saw that Grandpa was logged on.

J.O.E.: Evening, Eddie. I am typing this from a swimming pool.

I chatted to him for ages. He was in Italy, in a town that sounded a bit like San Jimmy Jammas. He had been walking all day and looking at lots of very old churches which sounded really boring, but the swimming pool bit sounded great. He told me that it was so hot that the only way to cool down was to sit on the steps of the pool. I told him about what had happened with Lexi and that I didn't know what to do.

J.O.E.: It's very simple. I think you know exactly what you have to do, don't you?

He was right, I did know, but before I said goodnight I had one more question that I'd wanted to ask for ages.

Eddie: What does the O in J.O.E. stand for? What's your middle name?

I knew his first name was Josiah but I'd never asked him about the O because I hate it when people ask me what my middle name is. It's ugly. I pretend that I don't have one.

J.O.E.: Well, now that would be telling, wouldn't it?

Of course that just made me want to know even more! I saw the green dot turn to red and I knew he was gone. I sat there for a while and even though Lexi wasn't logged on, I sent her this message:

> To: Lexiland@hotmail.com
> From: EddieE@hotmail.com
> Lexi,
> I am sorry. I am very, very sorry.
> Eddie
> P.S.
> My sister is trapped at the back of the wardrobe. Will you help me get her out?

21

On Friday I left for school a bit early so that I could be there when Lexi arrived. I walked up the hill – well, actually I sort of marched all the way up the hill – and now that it was summer I was really hot by the time I got to the bridge. I stopped, took off my jumper and wrapped it around my waist.

All the cars were beeping each other and I watched for a second to see why and saw that an old-fashioned car had broken down. It was blocking the entire bridge and a long queue of traffic had started to snake its way all the way back down the road.

The beeping got louder so I didn't hear her come up behind me.

LEXI: You counting the cars or something?

I turned around, smiled and noticed that she was wearing a new patch. It was dark blue not black and it seemed a bit smaller than the one she normally wore.

ME: I'm really sorry.

I couldn't tell if she was still upset with me so I sort of held my breath and waited. I just stared up at her hopefully. Then she sat down on the bench opposite the bridge, so I sat down too. She didn't say anything and I didn't say anything, but it was OK. She reached into her pocket and handed me a mint. We sat there for a while; the only sounds were crunching mints and beeping horns.

LEXI: Hannah says there's always one idiot who either breaks down on the bridge or doesn't have the right money to pay.

I looked at the long line of traffic. Hannah was right but then I remembered Dad's book.

ME: The bridge wasn't really designed for cars. It was designed for horse-drawn carriages but these days between ten and twelve thousand cars cross that bridge every single day. It's an amazing feat of engineering.

LEXI: It's just a bridge, Eddie. It does what all bridges do. It gets you from one side to the other. I mean, if it sort of slid you across, you know, like those cool slides you get at the fairground. I mean, if it did that, then it would be amazing.

She was right. Well, she was kind of right because a twisty, turning, sliding bridge would be more fun.

LEXI: Did you just remember that? I mean, is that your special memory thing?
ME: Yeah.
LEXI: Do ten thousand cars really cross it every day?
ME: Yep and it costs fifty pence to cross it so, that's about . . . five thousand pounds a day.
LEXI: Did you really just do that sum in your head? I wish I could do that.
ME: Well, I wish I had a music room.

I don't know why I said it. It just came out but ever since I'd been to LexiLand, I had been sort of wishing that I had a music room like Lexi or a house that had a banister that you could slide down, or a bedroom that had two beds, a sofa and a computer. Her house was *so* much more interesting than my little house. We didn't even have one garden, but Lexi had a front garden, a back garden, a roof garden *and* a hidden garden. Suddenly Lexi stood up, put her bag back on her shoulder and her hands on her hips.

LEXI: Well, are you going to tell me how we're going to get your sister out of the wardrobe or are you going to make me wait till tonight?

I jumped up, looped my arm into hers and as we walked across the Square I told her all about the conversation I had overheard. I told her my plan and she had some ideas of her own. She said it was a cunning plan but I laughed and told her, 'No, Lexi, it is a Canning Plan!'

*

Lexi and I left school together and as we walked back through the Square I started feeling a bit nervous because Lexi had never seen my house. As we neared the top of my road, I started to feel a bit funny. *What if she doesn't like it*, I thought? *What if she laughs at how small it is?* But as we turned into my road Lexi seemed more interested in the colour of the houses.

LEXI: Wow! Yellow, pink, purple, orange! I've never seen a street where the houses are all painted different colours! It must be like living in a rainbow.

I stopped outside number twelve. It was painted yellow.

LEXI: Look.

She pointed down the road at the row of multicoloured houses.

LEXI: It's so pretty! It really is like a rainbow and this road must be great for sledging.

I looked down the steep hill and I remembered the winter when it snowed a lot. There was so much snow that we couldn't get our car up the hill and everyone had to stay at home. When Rascoe saw the snow he didn't know what to do first. He tried to eat it, he tried to dig it and when everyone on the street had a massive snowball fight, he kept jumping up into the air to catch the snowballs in his mouth. It was great. Laura and I missed a day of school and Dad helped us to build a snowman outside the front door. Maybe my street was'nt so bad after all.

As soon as we got to my house, Mum opened the front door and Rory came rocketing out of the kitchen and threw his tiny arms around Lexi's legs.

RORY: Lexi! Lexi! Lexi!

Mum was really happy and chatty. She didn't moan about the pile of washing I could see in the laundry basket. She didn't huff and puff about the dishwasher or complain to Dad that she had to empty the bin again. She didn't ask me any stupid questions about school or homework. She didn't stare at nothing. She didn't shout at Rory when he put his hand inside the jar of mayonnaise and we even got to have an enormous takeaway pizza.

She smiled, she laughed and, for a little while, it was just like it used to be.

After we'd all eaten so much that it felt as though my tummy was going to burst, Dad lay down on the sofa and switched on the telly and Mum said she was going to give Rory his bath. I gave Lexi The Look. It was supposed to be a little wink but I ended up sort of blinking, winking and nodding all at the same time instead. Rory giggled and copied me. He tried to nod and wink and blink at the same time and Lexi thought it was hysterical. She picked him up again, his tiny legs wrapped around her waist like a baby and he rested his head on her shoulder.

RORY: I want you to bath me, Lexi.

I was just about to say no when Lexi turned to Mum and spoke first.

LEXI: Can I? Can I, please, Mrs Edwards?

Mum smiled.

MUM: Why not?

She looked at me.

MUM: See that, young lady? That's called helping.

I frowned as I watched Lexi take Rory to the foot of the stairs.

LEXI: OK, Rory, bet you can't get undressed by the time I get up there!

His face lit up with a big pizzary smile and he did a sort of happy dance. Mum and Lexi giggled. But I wasn't laughing. What about the plan? We were supposed to explore the wardrobe whilst Mum was dealing with Rory. Why was Lexi fussing over Rory just like Mum? Then before she went up the stairs, Lexi leant over to me, whispered something in my ear and I stopped worrying altogether. Instead I smiled and went to watch the telly with Dad.

Later, when we went to bed, Lexi spent ages looking at all the stuff in my room. She looked at the photographs of me and Laura and spent forever spinning the globe round and round. She told me that I was really lucky to have a little brother like Rory. She said she wished she wasn't an only child and that it would be much more fun to have a little brother or a sister. I thought about that for ages. Lucky to have a little brother? Maybe it was a bit lonely if it was just you. It would be like never having a Laura at all. She sat down on the beanbag, tucked her arms behind her head and asked me loads of questions like:

- How old was Laura when, you know? (Nine.)
- Who was born first? (Laura by eight and a half minutes.)
- How alike were we really? (Like looking in the mirror.)

211

As we were both yawning, we climbed into our beds. It felt a bit weird when I looked over and saw Lexi in Laura's bed. It made my tummy feel a bit strange. When Mum came in to say goodnight she stopped in the doorway and suddenly put her hand up to her mouth. I wondered if she felt a bit funny seeing someone else in Laura's bed too. She stood like that for a while until she heard Rory shouting from his bedroom and she went to check on him.

I turned on my side and saw that Lexi still had her patch on. I turned off the snow globe. I don't know why, but it felt as though I couldn't help myself from saying something.

ME: Are you going to sleep in your patch then?

It was dark but I could see that she was lying on her back looking up at all the luminous stars. She sighed and turned on her side.

LEXI: I did when I went to Greta's sleepover. I only really take it off at home.

I waited and waited for her to say something else, but then I heard the sound of heavy breathing and realised that she was asleep.

That night I had another horrible dream. I dreamt I was trapped inside a wardrobe and I could just see through the keyhole. There was a party on the other side, in a garden

212

with a large cake, and I really wanted to get out of the ward-robe and get to the party, but I couldn't open the door.

I woke up suddenly and sat bolt upright in my bed. My heart was racing and I could feel the sweat pouring down my back. Lexi was fast asleep, in fact she was almost doing Rory piglet snorts. The room was lit up by moonlight; it shone across her face and hair. Her curls seemed to glisten like coppery spirals and as I craned my neck to look I saw the patch in her hand. She had taken it off! I climbed out of bed slowly and leant across to look. She was lying on her side, sort of cuddling the pillow, so I could just see one side of her face but not the right side. I leaned a bit further forward and I could hear my heart beating quicker and quicker. *Thud–thud. Thud–thud.*

VOICE: Don't.

I stopped dead in my tracks. I sort of froze halfway.

VOICE: Don't.

I hovered in between the beds for a fraction of a second and then I quickly climbed back into my bed. Had Lexi heard the voice too? I listened but I could just hear the sound of her sleeping breath and the *thud–thud* of my heart.

*

The next morning I woke up to the sound of beeping horns and clattering trains. I turned over quickly, but Lexi was gone and as I followed the noises downstairs I saw why. She was sitting playing trains with Rory, but this time I didn't mind at all. In fact, I went over to the rug, sat with them and the three of us built an enormous train track until Mum came down to make us breakfast.

After we had eaten eggs, bacon, toast and cereal, it was time to put our plan into action. And this time it didn't involve any silly winking, blinking or nodding of heads. Lexi had a much, much better plan. If I was to get to the back of the wardrobe and get Laura out, we needed to do some of the best pretending ever. Our plan was foolproof and it involved maths, Lexi's brilliant acting and me creeping around as quietly as I could. I looked at Lexi and gave the signal: two little coughs. Then she bent down to Rory and whispered into his ear. He immediately jumped up, ran into the hall and returned, moments later with his red wellington boots.

RORY: Park! Wanna! Please.

At the same time, I leant down and placed a bit of bacon on Dad's slipper. Rascoe was on it before I had a chance to sit up again, but when he saw the red wellingtons he started wagging his tail, spinning in circles and barking.

RORY: Walkies, Wascoe! Walkies!

Rascoe ran around the table, into the hall and came skidding back into the room with the lead in his mouth.

214

MUM: Great idea, Rory! Why don't we all go? Girls?

I nudged Lexi under the table so she put down her fork and turned to Mum.

LEXI: Mrs Edwards?
MUM: Please call me Fiona. I feel like I'm at school if people call me Mrs Edwards; it's my grown-up teacher name.
LEXI: Well, that's what I wanted to ask you about because you're a maths teacher and I, well, I'm not . . .

Lexi put her head in her hands and started to cry like she had done that day in the toilets.

LEXI: I can't . . . do . . . maths . . . and Miss Cauber . . . gets really . . . cross . . . with . . . me . . . and . . .

But Mum was already up and out of her seat kneeling down in front of Lexi. I tried not to giggle but Lexi was pretty amazing at acting and Mum totally fell for it.

MUM: Would you like me to help? I used to help Laura, didn't I, Em?
ME: Eddie!
MUM: I used to help your sister, didn't I, *Eddie*?
ME: Yeah, but it's Saturday. Lexi doesn't want to have a maths lesson on a Saturday, do you?
LEXI: But I really would, if that's OK?

So Dad took Rory and Rascoe to the park and Lexi pretended that doing fractions at the kitchen table with my mum was just what she wanted to do and I pretended I wasn't very pleased. I did a pretend stomp upstairs and then waited on the landing. After a while I heard Mum's school-teacher voice say, 'Lexi, imagine a pie cut into four slices. See that? That's one part of the whole. If I take one of them, I have taken one of the four. One quarter. See? I can write it like this.'

As soon as I heard that, I knew I was safe. I walked across the hallway to Mum and Dad's bedroom and slowly pushed open the door. I could feel my stomach flip over and my heart beat quicker. *Thud-thud. Thud-thud.* I walked over to the wardrobe and for a long time I just stood very still. *Thud-thud. Thud-thud.*

22

The first Christmas without Laura was horrible, but I did get a present which I loved. It was a book. It was a story about a little girl who discovers a magical world hidden at the back of the wardrobe. Not long after that, I went to Grandma's house and found a wardrobe which was full of old coats: Mum's old school blazer, a long green felt coat with a strange-looking hood, a shiny red raincoat, a black puffy one that didn't have any sleeves and lots and lots of scarves. For a long time I used to check that wardrobe just in case it led to another world. I used to pretend I needed the toilet and then I'd sneak into the spare bedroom, slowly open the door and hope every time that I'd find my very own magical world. As my hands reached in and my fingers tentatively felt past the coats, I wished that there might just be a special place that I could run away to, but there never was.

As I stood in front of my parents' wardrobe, I rested my forehead against the door and took two deep breaths.

My heart was still beating really quickly. *Thud-thud. Thud-thud*, as I turned the little key and opened the doors. They opened without any creaking or squeaking, just sort of swung outwards towards me. The first thing I did was look behind the shoe boxes. More shoes, lots of shoes, lots of shoes I had never seen Mum wear before and Laura was right, Dad's trainers *were* really stinky. I looked through the rack of trousers and blouses, through the piles of jumpers and cardigans. I looked in the drawer where Mum keeps her bras and through the mountain of lonely socks and ties. There was one tie which caught my eye. It was black and miserable-looking. It was a horrible tie that I could only remember my dad wearing once. I picked it up and for some reason I held it up to my face and smelt it. *Dad.* It smelt of Dad so I looped it around my neck and felt around behind the scary Christmas tree decoration dress. I reached out and the tip of my finger felt something cold. It was cold and hard and seemed very, very small. I picked it up and pulled it out of the wardrobe.

It was a small, ugly vase.

I ran my finger along its smooth lid and sat down on the bed. It was a vase not much bigger than the one I'd seen at Lexi's. But I knew this vase wasn't for exotic flowers or daffodils picked from the garden.

It was an urn.

It was *my sister's* urn and inside it were her ashes.

I suddenly felt really sad all over again. It felt as though I was being told for the first time that Laura was gone. As I put my hands around the urn, I could hear Mum and Dad on that horrible, horrible day. It was as though they were telling me that Laura was dead, it was as if it was happening all over again.

I looked up at the wardrobe and kicked the doors shut. Laura wasn't really here. My *Laura* wasn't really at the back of the wardrobe, just her ugly little urn. I looked down at the silver plaque.

Laura Edwards 2003–2012

I sat there for a while and remembered the day that Mum and Dad had tried to explain what was going to happen to Laura now that she was gone. They had tried to get me to understand that a person can be buried or cremated and when they told me my sister was going to be cremated I had cried and cried.

Grandma had tried to help by telling me about the grandfather that I had never met. He died before Laura and I were born. Grandma told me that Grandfather had been ill, he'd been sick for a very long time and he'd told her that when he died he wanted his ashes to be taken to his favourite spot. So, one summer's evening, Grandma had taken him down to the river where he used to fish. She drove his little urn all the way down to Devon and walked across three fields of long wavy grass, climbed over stiles, through muddy ditches and nettles, bracken and brambles, she even got stung by a horsefly, until finally she found Grandfather's favourite fishing spot, their secret place. And there, at the bend in the river, she tipped his ashes into the water, so he'd always be at his favourite place. So he'd always be at *their* special spot and so that Grandma, Mum and Aunt Shelly had somewhere very beautiful to go and visit him. Somewhere, that was filled with happy memories. Memories of Grandfather catching his very first salmon and of Mum and Aunt Shelly paddling in the water when they were little and of moonlit picnics under the stars. But I didn't want to tip Laura's ashes anywhere so I held them tightly, lay down on the bed, and curled myself around them.

The next thing I knew Rory had jumped on the bed and was shaking the ugly little vase like a castanet.

RORY: What is it? What is it?

Before I had a chance to do anything, he jumped off the bed and ran out of the room carrying Laura with him. I chased after him into the hallway, but he was gone.

At the bottom of the stairs, standing in front of the door was my dad. My soaking wet dad.

DAD: It's pouring down out there. We only got as far as the cheese car. We had to make a dash for it, didn't we, Ror? Rory? Where's he gone?

I didn't know what to do. I felt sort of stuck to the spot. I panicked. Then I heard a giggle and Rory shot out of the bathroom and ran down the stairs and in his left hand was Laura. He was waving the urn above his head like a football trophy.

RORY: Look! Look! I got it!

Dad's mouth dropped open and he froze. I didn't move either. There was a moment when the two of us knew, when we both felt the same. It was a terrible, dawning horror. Rory ran past Dad and into the kitchen and we both knew we had to get the urn out of his hands and we had to do it quickly.

DAD: Roreeeeeeeee!
ME: Roreeeeeeeee!

I think I ran down the stairs, but I don't remember my feet touching any of the steps. Then I followed Dad who had chased Rory into the kitchen.

Rory climbed up on to the seat by the window and jumped up and down.

RORY: I got it! I want it!

Mum and Lexi stopped dividing pies into neat little fractions and looked very confused. Then Mum saw what Rory was waving and she jumped up from the table, ran over to the seat and tried to grab his feet.

MUM: Give me that now!
DAD: Come down from there, Rory! THIS IS NOT A GAME!

They were shouting and screaming at him and Lexi and I ran round the kitchen table and tried to help.

LEXI: Rory, get down.
ME: Give me that now, you bloody stupid little squirt!

But Rory kept waving the urn above his head. I tried to grab him and he lifted his foot up. My dad tried to get hold of him and he squashed himself against the bookcase of cookery books. Even Lexi tried to catch him, but Rory wriggled and giggled and squirmed this way and that way and we all watched in horror as his other hand reached for the lid. He reached for the lid and tugged.

MUM: RORY, NO!

He twisted the lid.

DAD: RORY, NO!

He tugged at the lid.

ME: ROREEEEEEEEEEEEEEEEEEEEEE, NO!

There was a loud popping sound and everything seemed to slow down. There was a loud popping sound and a cloud of grey ash formed in the air above us. Lexi ducked and Mum tried to catch it in her jumper, my dad just stared up into the air watching my sister's ashes fall all around us on to the floor.

The soft grey ash settled on the rug, on the sofa, on the chair, on the table, on the pictures. Everywhere. *Laura was everywhere.*

I watched the ashes falling around me, *upon* me. She was in my hair, on my clothes and on my skin. I saw the tiny grey flecks, smaller than the freckles on Lexi's nose, but I didn't hear a sound. I didn't hear Mum screaming for the dustpan and brush. I didn't hear my Dad shout at Rory or hear him crying.

I turned around and even though I was covered in my sister's ashes, I walked slowly up to my bedroom and shut the door.

As I walked into the bedroom I heard a clunking sound. I looked over at Laura's bed and saw something sticking out from underneath it. I bent down to look. It was our Super-Secret book. I don't know how it got under Laura's bed. Maybe I had knocked it off the wardrobe when I fell off the table.

I picked it up, sat down on Laura's bed and closed my eyes. It wasn't long before the bedroom door opened. It was Mum. I turned away from her.

MUM: You need to . . . you need to wash it off.

I looked up at her. She still had some ash on her face and on her cardigan. I looked at her and shouted.

ME: **NO! I AM NOT EVER GOING TO WASH AGAIN! EVER! EVER! LEAVE ME ALONE!**

She stared at me for a while and then disappeared downstairs again.

She left me. Just like she always did.

I gripped our Super-Secret book and hugged my knees.

I didn't hear Mum come back.

I didn't hear her say my name softly and gently just like she used to do.

She knelt down in front of me and I could see she was crying. In one hand she had the ugly little urn and in the other a small silver brush. It was a soft silver baby brush that was no bigger than my hand. It was my silver baby brush.

I looked up at Mum's hand and then into her eyes. She leaned towards me and my eyes didn't move from hers.

With one hand she brushed the ash off my jumper and back into the urn. I felt the delicate bristles gently sweep away the ash. *Brush, brush, brush.* From my arms, my hair, my face. *Brush. Brush. Brush.* Mum looked at me and with one hand she tucked a strand of hair behind my ear, with the other she raised the silver baby brush up to her lips and kissed the back of it.

MUM: I love you, my little one.

I looked at her without breathing and then I felt her arms around me, surrounding me. I tucked my head into the warmth of her side and I breathed again. She held me tightly, I held her tightly and I didn't ever want to let go.

MUM: I'm so sorry. I couldn't decide. I didn't know what to do. Your grandfather had a special place, he wanted to be taken to the river. But I don't know what Laura would want. I don't know what to do.

I turned my head slightly and out of the corner of my eye I saw our Special-Secret book. I picked it up and showed Mum the things that nobody but Laura and I had seen. As we turned the pages, one picture caught my eye. I don't know why but I had a sort of idea and I was going to say something, but I changed my mind and then I learnt something new.

I learnt that sometimes you can be really sad and really happy, all at the same time. Because when Mum saw all the drawings that Laura had done, when we turned the pages together, she was smiling and crying.

We both were.

23

Mum and I were still sitting on Laura's bed laughing at my silly stories, when Lexi came into the bedroom. In one of her hands was a pair of scissors and in the other was a strand of her hair. Well, it was more of a lock of hair. It was a chunk of red hair.

LEXI: Here.

Mum and I looked up at the red noodle dangling in front of us.

LEXI: Look. It's still a bit . . . you know? It's still got . . . you know?

I leant forward and could see that the lock of hair really was a little bit grey. I held out my hand and she dropped it into my left palm.

MUM: I have an idea.

She disappeared downstairs and when she came back she had in her hand a glue stick and a small white envelope. Mum picked up the Super-Secret book and turned it to the back. She turned it to the back and turned it upside down, just like I'd shown her. She looked at me and winked. I knew exactly what she was going to do. She put the lock of red ashy hair inside the small white envelope, turned to a fresh page, glued it inside and above it she wrote:

Saturday May 25th
The Third Twin.

When Hannah came to pick Lexi up, she spent ages chatting to Mum and I watched them from the top of the stairs. Hannah gave Mum a box of what looked like biscuits and when she said something to her, they both laughed and hugged each other. Mum looked up at me and smiled.

Later that night I helped Mum with Rory. I washed his hair, making sure I didn't get soap suds in his eyes, played with the little ducks and sang his favourite frog song. He didn't cry or moan, not even once.

ME: Did I like bath times when I was little?

Mum looked at me with surprise.

MUM: You! Ha! You think Rory kicks up a fuss! You hated it. You once hid underneath our bed just so I couldn't find you. And you once did a poo in the bath just so I had to let all the water out.

I loved Mum telling me what I was like, especially if I was a bit naughty.

MUM: Yep, you were a monster about getting your hair wet.

She lifted Rory out of the bath and wrapped him in a huge fluffy white towel.

I laughed and watched Mum rub Rory dry. He liked this bit. It made him go all giggly. Laura was just the same. I would wrap my towel around my shoulders and sit on the carpet but Laura would climb on to Mum's knee so she could 'rub-a-dub-dub' her dry. She'd laugh and say, 'Faster, Mummy, faster!' I remembered our bath times really well. We always had a bath together and Laura would make me sit by the taps. She would always sit opposite me. Face to face.

I tried to see her smile, but I couldn't. I closed my eyes. I could see her wrapped up in a towel. I could see her head and her legs but when I tried to see her face I couldn't! I couldn't remember. I was forgetting her. I couldn't hear her laughter. Her giggles were gone. Her grin was disappearing from my memory. I suddenly stood up and looked at Mum.

ME: I can't remember! I can't remember her smile. I can't remember how she smelt. It's going. It's going!

I felt my heart beating quickly again and the tears rolled down my cheeks. I ran into my bedroom, lay down on Laura's bed, squashed my face into her pillow and I tried to smell her again but there was no smell. She was fading!

A moment later both Mum and Dad came into the room. I turned over. Dad sat down on my bed and Mum knelt down towards me. Her hand was at her throat touching the silver heart-shaped locket that Dad had given her for her birthday and as I sat up, she unfastened the necklace and took it off.

MUM: Look.

She held out the silver locket and I watched as she opened the tiny heart. I watched as she unfolded the miniature photograph frame that was hiding inside it. She held it up to my face and I saw three small pictures. Silly Laura. Smiling Laura. Sulking Laura. I knew the last one. I remembered it really well. It was taken on the beach. We had been on holiday and when it was time to go Laura had screamed the beach down.

ME: The beach.

Mum smiled and Dad passed her an orange-coloured bottle. A bottle of sun lotion. She opened the lid and held it under my nose so that I could breathe in the lovely coconut smell. I closed my eyes and breathed in the sweet scent. *Coconut, sand and the sound of crashing waves.* I breathed in the lovely smell and I saw Laura's face once more.

ME: Laura!

I closed my eyes and I saw her. I saw her smile, I heard her voice. I heard her say, '*I will not ever, ever leave. This is MY beach.*'

MUM: Sometimes it can feel sad to remember, but it can also help us to be happy again . . . Can you remember what happened?

I nodded. I *could* remember. And for the first time I let myself remember *that* day. Before, I'd always stopped myself. If I was at Grandma's house, if I was in the garden and I suddenly started to think of it, I would tell myself, '*NO! DON'T! STOP IT!*' But now I let myself remember. I closed my eyes and saw it all.

Our last birthday was in Grandma's garden. The sun was warm and pale and yellow. There were flowers everywhere. The sky was

230

the bluest blue. There was a bouncy castle, the smell of grass and everyone was there. Mum wore silver shoes and a dress with polka dots. Dad had a red nose and a stripy purple hat. Music was playing loudly, Rory was being Rory and we were hot as hot. Laura and I were jumping. Laura shouted, 'Higher!' We were jumping up together. We were bouncing in our castle. Grandpa had his camera. 'Look this way, girls. Smile for me. Look this way,' he said. Aunt Shelly was chasing Rory, her lips were painted red.

Then we were running. We were racing to the table. There were plates of food and piles of opened presents.

There was a birthday cake. There were candles and everyone was singing.

'Happy Birthday to you! Happy Birthday to you two!'

'A slice for me.'

'A slice for you.'

I had frosting on my nose. Laura had frosting in her hair. We had frosting on our fingers. There was chocolate everywhere.

'I can eat mine quicker.'

'My slice is bigger.'

I was laughing. Laura was laughing. Then she wasn't.

I was smiling. Laura was smiling. Then she wasn't.

Her hands came up towards her face. The piece of cake she'd been holding landed on my foot.

Her hands went to her throat. Somebody was screaming. Someone else was shouting. I saw Laura's eyes flicker and then she tipped backwards to the ground.

Suddenly everyone was running towards us and shouting. They crowded all around her and I couldn't see her face any more.

I couldn't see her. I couldn't hear her. A siren was wailing. A noise so loud it hurt. The ambulance. The stretcher. Laura!

She was gone.

Mum and Dad went with her, but when they came back home again, they came back home without her.

She was gone.

'Where is she?' I shouted at them. 'Where is she? Where's my Laura?'

Then they told me. And when they told me, I wanted to shout and scream at them. I cried and cried and I said, 'I don't believe you! Go and get her!' Mum just started sobbing and I wanted to say, 'Shut up! Stop it! Bring my Laura home or go away!'

*

We had to go and say goodbye. I didn't want to. I said I wouldn't. I screamed and I shouted at them. I didn't want to say goodbye to Laura. They told me to take something. Mum said I could bring something. 'Bring something for Laura,' she said, 'bring something she loved.'

For a long time I just lay on her bed and cried so much my head hurt. When it was time to go, Dad had to pick me up and carry me to the car, but I still had my favourite bear in my hand.

Mum sat in the back with me and Grandma drove us to the place where Laura was. But when we saw her, it didn't look like Laura at all. She was so still and pale and I held my breath waiting, wishing and hoping that any second, any moment, she would open up her eyes.

It was Laura but it wasn't. She was there but she wasn't and I left my favourite bear beside her.

ME: She was there. Then she was gone.

DAD: I know. I know. It happened so quickly.

Mum held my hand over the locket.

MUM: It was her heart. It didn't work properly. It . . .

She took my left hand and held it to her chest.

MUM: It didn't beat properly.

I felt Mum's heartbeat. *Thud. Thud. Thud.*

DAD: And on that day it just stopped beating. It couldn't work any more.

I sat up quickly, my eyes wide, my skin prickled. I sat bolt upright and looked back at them.

ME: So it wasn't her fault? It wasn't the silly cake or anything?

MUM: No.

DAD: No, it wasn't her fault.

I went over to the bookcase and picked up the photograph of me and Laura.

ME: Sorry, Laura. Sorry, I know it wasn't your fault now. Sorry and I miss you.

I kissed the photograph and put it back on the shelf, but then I remembered Rory's birthday and horrid sorbet cake.

ME: But why did we have to have a weird sorbet cake for Rory's birthday?

They looked at each other and burst out laughing. Mum got up, sat down next to Dad and he put his arms around her.

DAD: We didn't *have* to have a sorbet cake. We didn't *have* to have one, you silly thing!
MUM: Your little brother *wanted* one.

Dad rolled his eyes.

DAD: Yeah, thanks to your grandma!
MUM: She was trying to teach him all about melting and freezing.

Dad laughed.

DAD: Can you believe it, Eddie – he was having his first science lesson?

I thought of Grandma and her constant 'doing' and 'learning'. Grandma would *always* be a head teacher.

MUM: Anyway, the day before, your grandma let him try sorbet for the very first time and from that moment on it was all he wanted to eat. Don't you remember?

And I did. I suddenly remembered because that was the time when Rory couldn't actually say 'S' properly. He couldn't say sausages or sorry. He could only say 'hossages' and 'horry'. So he couldn't even say sorbet either. It was a sort of 'horr-bay'.

DAD: So, he just *had* to have it for his birthday as well.
MUM: He insisted. At first we said no. Your Grandma had already made the cake. I think it was a train-shaped cake or something but it had to be a 'horr-bay' cake . . . He really roared about that one.

Of course! How could I have forgotten? Rory's birthday! I had been really grumpy all day. I hadn't wanted to come downstairs for his little party. Of course! I remembered the funny-looking square lumps and the melting mess in the kitchen.

DAD: Well, we tried. We tried to make it look more like a birthday cake, didn't we, Fi?

Mum laughed.

MUM: Hmm, well it certainly looked like a something.

<u>At bedtime</u>
I was just turning to chapter eleven when Mum came in and sat down on the bean bag.

MUM: Hannah is really lovely, isn't she?
ME: Yeah. She's kind of different.
MUM: You know, I didn't have many friends when I was at school. I wasn't . . . you know, good at making friends. Your Aunt Shelly was always making new friends, she still is. But I guess . . . maybe you and I are a bit alike.

It was the first time that she'd ever told me.

MUM: I still find it hard to make friends but . . .
ME: Do you think you will be friends with Hannah?

She got up and sat down on my bed.

MUM: I hope so.

I did too and I lay back on the pillow and smiled.

MUM: It's a bank holiday on Monday.

I'd forgotten all about it.

MUM: Would you like to stay at Lexi's house tomorrow?

My eyes widened.

ME: Overnight? A sleepover?
MUM: Yes. If you want to.

I sat up and hugged her again.

ME: Thank you.

*

The next day I woke up early and Mum helped me pack my bag.
I was so excited; it was a bit like Christmas used to be. Mum
walked me up the hill, through the park and along the wide tree-
lined road to the zoo but when I showed her the narrow
passageway she said she knew all about it. At Canning Circus,
Lexi and Hannah were already waiting and as I got closer to Lexi
I saw her hold up a large metal key. I knew exactly what it was for.

LEXI: Come on! Leave your bags here. We're going to
have a picnic.

Hannah took my bag and she and Mum disappeared through
the shiny black door.

LEXI: Eddie! Come on!

237

She'd already turned down the path towards the hidden garden so I ran after her. I waited while she fiddled with her patch and tried to unlock the gate at the same time. I tried to peer over her head but it was impossible to see anything but branches. Then the gate opened with a loud squeaking sound and we both stepped inside. The garden was much bigger than I had imagined. I stood still and looked all around me. The grass was freshly mown so that the air was filled with a sweet grassy smell. Some of the trees hung down low over the lawn and all around its edges were lots of different and brightly coloured flowers.

LEXI: Look.

She ran ahead up to the top of the garden and disappeared behind the back of a large flowerbed. I ran after her and as I turned round the side of a huge purple rhododendron, I saw that there was another part of the garden that was hidden.

LEXI: It's like a secret garden inside a hidden garden, isn't it?

It was, but it was even prettier than the rest of the garden and that was where Lexi and I laid out our picnic rug and sat down. After a while Hannah and Mum came and joined us.

I was lying down chatting to Lexi, but every so often I turned to look at Mum and she was laughing loudly and doing that thing where she waves her hands around in the air when she chats. She was being different, more like she used to be smiling all the time and once she looked over and blew me a kiss. And I did what I always used to do. I pretended to catch it.

When it was time for Mum to leave, she hugged me tightly and whispered in my ear.

MUM: You're the greenest apple and I'm the apple tree.
ME: I'm just a little fish and . . .
MUM: I am the deep blue sea.

She bent down and kissed the tip of my nose.

MUM: Have a lovely time.

And I did. I had the most amazing time.

We had spaghetti for dinner and I listened to Hannah tell me how she'd lived in Paris, Rome, New York and Australia. She told me that she had danced on stages all over the world. That she had danced and danced until one day her feet didn't want to do any more dancing and she had to think of something else to do.

HANNAH: When I'm not being a mum, I sort of make things . . . you know pots and jugs and bowls and things. I'll show you tomorrow. You know, when I was at school, I tried to be good at maths and science but I found it

really hard and when we did things like art, which I loved
– adored – I couldn't even draw a stick-man. So darling,
Eddie, in the end I can only ever be what I really am.

And when I asked her what that was she just laughed. I told
Hannah about the 'something' that I had made for the art
corner and that no one knew what it was, but she just
laughed and leant over to me, cupping my face in her ringed
hands.

HANNAH: Oh, Eddie. That is perfect. You know what?
You didn't make a 'something' – it was better than that.
Do you know what it was?
ME: Not really, I just liked the way the clay felt when I
squished it about.
HANNAH: If they couldn't work out what it was, that
means only one thing.
ME: What?
HANNAH: It means it was different. It means it stood out
from the rest.

I grinned. *Different.* For once I quite liked the sound of that.
Hannah lifted her glass up to her mouth, took a big gulp of
wine, stood up very quickly, sort of pirouetted across the
kitchen floor and bowed.

HANNAH: Eddie, you're an artist!

Lexi and I laughed. Hannah was so unlike any other grown up I had ever met and I watched with delight as she fished a huge tub of ice cream out of the freezer for us all to share.

When it was time to go to bedtime I was so tired that I almost forgot that this was my first ever sleepover. When Lexi turned out the light I noticed that she still had her patch on. I thought about what Lexi had told me about the sleepover at Greta's and I took a deep breath and asked the question I'd wanted to ask for ages:

ME: What happened at Greta's? What did she do?

Lexi sighed and didn't say anything for ages.

LEXI: When I went into her bathroom to wash my face, Greta sneaked in behind me and took my patch away from me. She wouldn't give it me back. She said she wouldn't give it me back until I showed her.
ME: And did you? I mean, did you have to?
LEXI: No. I just covered my face and screamed at her. I screamed at her until her mum came running up the stairs and when she saw what Greta was doing, she marched over to her and shouted at her really loudly and Greta dropped my patch and burst into tears.

I lay there for ages thinking about it.

LEXI: Hannah says it can be really horrid if your parents get divorced. She said that Greta is probably really sad that her dad went to live somewhere else. Hannah says it's not really her fault that she gets all mean.

I snuggled down under the duvet and after a few wriggles this way and that way I decided that Lexi's guest bed was a lot more squidgy than my bed at home.

LEXI: Eddie?
ME: Yes.
LEXI: Why did you cut all your hair off?

At first I didn't know what to say and I tried to remember the day when it happened. Mum and Dad were rowing and I had got so fed up and so angry that I just . . .

ME: I was really cross with my mum.
LEXI: Why?
ME: I don't really know any more.
LEXI: I get that sometimes. Sometimes, I get really monster-angry about something. Hannah says we both have a really bad temper and Dad says that when we both get going, we look like we're going to breathe fire or something.

Like dragons, I thought.

24

The next morning Hannah made us a breakfast I had never eaten before. When we came down to the kitchen it smelt like a bakery and on the long wooden table there was a pile of thick pancakes, maple syrup and a plate of smoky, crispy bacon rashers. Hannah handed me a glass of orange juice, dropped the little white tablet into the palm of my hand and went out into the garden to hang out the washing.

LEXI: What's that?
ME: Oh, it's my 'keep you fit and strong' tablet.
LEXI: What? You mean a vitamin?

She leant across the table and snatched it out of my hand.

LEXI: That's not a vitamin! That's medicine.

She went over to the window to look at it closer and I don't know why but it made me feel quite cross with her.

ME: Give it back to me!

But Lexi just turned the tablet over in her hand.

LEXI: This is medicine. I should know! I've had to take lots of it before.

I jumped down from my seat and went over to where she was standing.

ME: Just give it me back, will you? You don't know what you're talking about! They're just to keep you fit and strong. You don't know everything, Lexi Lister!

I snatched the tablet from her hand.

LEXI: Hey! You know you don't have to be so grumpy, Eddie. I'm just saying.
ME: Yeah, well, you're always 'just saying', aren't you?

Lexi put her hands on her hips and shrugged.

LEXI: It's not my fault you don't know! But I do! THAT is not a vitamin!

ME: You're such a know-it-all, Lexi!

LEXI: And you're just being stupid, stupid, stupid!

ME: And you have a really, really big mouth. A really loud, really bossy, big mouth!

We just stood there for a second staring at each other.

LEXI: Well, you know what to do, if you don't like it, don't you?!

ME: Yes! I do and I don't need you to tell me!

And with that I ran out of the kitchen and up the first flight of stairs, but as I climbed up the next step, I had a funny feeling, like I'd done this all before. And as I got to the top of the stairs I realised that this was just like me and Laura! It was the same but kind of different too.

When me and Laura used to fight, Mum used to call them our 'silly squabbles'. I knew that if this *was* just like the arguments I had with Laura, then I had to do what I always *used* to do. I had to wait until Lexi came to find me. I stood outside the door to the drawing room and waited, but Lexi didn't come. I slowly walked into the room and sat down on the big red sofa and waited. But Lexi didn't come then either. After a while, I noticed that the door to the music room was open, so I got up and quietly crept across the room and through the door. It was just as I remembered. I sat down at the stool and lifted up the lid. I looked around the room at all the posters and the one above the little desk of *The Moon and the Star and the King of Omar* caught my eye. The music came into my head first and I heard Laura's voice singing, just like when we were coming home on the train. I lifted my hand up to the keys and they hovered there for a moment before I started to play. It was a simple tune and my grandma had taught me how to play it. It was easy, and it sounded so lovely on Lexi's beautiful piano. I played it so gently that my fingers just brushed the keys.

Then I heard Lexi thundering up the stairs. I heard her thudding up each one, but I didn't stop playing. I heard her rush into the room and crash into the foldaway doors, but I didn't stop playing. And then I felt her behind me, but I didn't stop playing. Lexi didn't speak. She didn't shout at me in her loud Lexi voice. Instead she sang along softly, so quietly that it was almost like a whisper.

LEXI: *Dreams they can be wonderful, they are magic in the night, where everything is special and beautiful and bright.*

Then she stopped, sat down next to me and rested her head upon my shoulder.

LEXI: My dad used to sing that to me.

My fingers hung above the keys.

LEXI: When I was in the hospital. After the operations. When I was in-between sleeping and being awake. Or if it hurt so bad that I couldn't even cry. He used to sing that to me.

I let my hands rest on my lap.

LEXI: He used to sing that to me every time.

We stayed like that for a while and then Hannah shouted up at us that she was going in The Studio and Lexi suddenly jumped up and grabbed my hand.

LEXI: Come on, I want to show you something!

We ran through the house and to the garden room. It was a funny-looking building at the bottom of the back garden. From the outside it just looked like an overgrown doll house, but inside it was like a treasure chest.

Hannah was sat at her drawing table using a massive magnifying glass and painting a tiny little box no bigger than a matchbox.

Lexi showed me all the beautiful things that they had made together: a large dish with blue and green fishes, a vase with gold and silver stripes, a milk jug that was painted the same colour as my mum's favourite necklace. On the middle shelf was a small rectangular box. I picked it up and saw that the whole thing was painted to look like the sea and on each side were curling waves, starfish, sea horses and other fish. On the top there was a larger gold fish which stuck out of the box to make a sort of lid and when I lifted the gold fish off the box I could see a very small round hole.

LEXI: Look inside.

I lifted the turquoise box to my face and peered inside the hole. Lexi tilted it to one side and I saw a golden star shoot past the hole.

ME: Wow!
LEXI: It's cool, isn't it? That's my favourite.

I did it again and two stars flew past the hole.

ME: How did you get the stars inside?

Hannah looked up from her desk.

HANNAH: I couldn't possibly tell you that. Maybe a little magic.

I put the gold fish lid back on and turned the box over and over in my hands. Each time I could hear the faint rattle of the wooden stars inside and on the back in tiny white letters I read, *Painted Sea*.

Lexi picked up a pretty yellow bowl and held it up.

LEXI: I made this when I came out of hospital.

I waited for her to tell me more but she didn't, so I bent down to the bookcase and looked along the spines. Underneath all the pretty vases, plates and bowls was a row of books. I read all the spines, Picasso, Dali, Bacon, Gauguin, Miro, Modernism, Minimalism, Baroque. One book was called *The Anthology of Names* and it was almost as big as a telephone book. Inside it was like a dictionary that listed all the names that had ever been from A to Z and it told you what they meant.

Of course Lexi had to be the first. She grabbed it from me and turned to her name: Alexandria.

LEXI: Look. Defender of mankind! But my first middle name . . .
ME: Your *first* middle name?
LEXI: Yeah, as if Alexandria wasn't stupid enough they gave me three more ridiculous names. On my birth certificate I am Alexandria Ruth Ursula Andrea Lister. But I will always be just Lexi. Lexi Lister.
ME: You have three middle names?
LEXI: I know, it's completely stupid and my dad says that my initials look like an eye chart. Look.

She picked up a scrap of paper and drew her initials. I looked down at the letters and for a second I thought they looked funny but then she plucked the paper from my fingers.

LEXI: So what's your middle name?

ME: I'm not telling you, it's ugly.

Hannah looked up from her desk.

HANNAH: Who told you that?

ME: Greta, she said my middle name is ugly.

HANNAH: That is such rubbish, Eddie! Ignore that girl.

LEXI: Well? What is it? Now I *have* to know.

ME: I'm named after my Great Aunt Eve.

Lexi laughed.

LEXI: Sorry, so your initials are E.E.E?

ME: No, Eve is short for something. Eve is what everyone called her, but it's short for Yvette.

Neither of them said anything but I just thought they were thinking, '*Poor you, that really is an ugly middle name.*' Then Hannah suddenly stood up from her desk and ran over to us. She showed Lexi a piece of paper and she gasped.

ME: What's wrong? What's the matter? I know it's ugly, you can say. I pretend I don't have a middle name. I've even crossed it out on my birth certificate.

LEXI: Look! Look!

She held the scrap of white paper under my nose. I looked down at the writing. Hannah had written some letters. At the top of the page she had written Lexi's initials:

A.R.U.A.L

And underneath it she had written them again but backwards:

L.A.U.R.A

My mouth dropped open and my stomach flipped over as I stared at the letters again, and I turned to look up at Hannah but she was pointing at the bottom of the page. She was pointing at some other writing. She was pointing at my initials. Her paint-flecked finger was pointing at this:

E.Y.E

I looked up at her face and I felt all the hairs on my body stand on end. I felt sort of tingly all over.

HANNAH: That is quite something, eh, Lexi?

I looked at the letters again.

E.Y.E.

I looked at the letters and felt my heart beat quicker, and quicker, then Lexi took my hand in hers.

LEXI: Come with me. I'm ready to show you now.

She stood up, I followed her to the window and she turned to face me.

LEXI: Promise you won't go all weird on me.

I couldn't speak so she turned her back and I watched her hands come up to the back of her head. They disappeared into the curly red hair and my heart beat a little faster when I saw the dark blue patch fall to the ground. *Thud-thud. Thud-thud. Flutter-flutter. Flutter-flutter.* She slowly turned to face me and I saw the whole of her face for the very first time. She tilted her head at an angle so that the sunlight shone brightly across her freckly cheeks and I saw that the tiny scar I had once seen was actually a very long scar. It was as long as the palm of my hand. It started at the top of her eyebrow and went diagonally across her eyelid to the far corner of her eye. It wasn't reddish or pink. It didn't look painful or sore. Instead it was silvery and it almost glistened in the light. I could see Lexi was breathing quickly and as she opened her eyes I saw her hands clench into fists. But her eyelids didn't open at the same time. Her right eyelid flickered and slowly closed again. I looked at the silvery scar, reached out my left hand and with the tip of my left index finger I touched it. She let out a long deep sigh and I watched a tear run down her cheek but she was smiling.

LEXI: Don't worry, silly. I'm not really crying. It doesn't really work properly, you know. It's not a real eye.

I looked at her eye again and this time she looked right at me. This time she was looking at me with both eyes.

LEXI: They're making me a new one, aren't they, Hannah?

I turned to Hannah who was sitting with her hands pressed to her mouth.

HANNAH: They are indeed.
LEXI: Apparently it's really hard to match the colour. It's really hard to get the same green.

I looked again and saw that while her left eye moved, her right eye did not.

HANNAH: Are you going to stay patch free?

Lexi frowned at her and sighed.

LEXI: I haven't decided.

Then she took my hand and pulled me away from the window.

LEXI: Come on. Let's go back to the house and find something fun to do!

She ran out of the garden room and across the lawn, but her navy blue patch stayed where it was, on the floor by the window in the garden room.

From then on Lexi wore her patch when we went out and at school, but whenever we got to LexiLand and it was just us at Canning Circus, the first thing she'd do was pull it off and throw it on the table in the hall where it would land below the mirror, in the shimmering hallway, in the middle of all the silver photograph frames.

25

Later that day Mum came to pick me up and we walked back through the village, chatting all the way.

I told her all about the yummy breakfast and the studio that was filled with the prettiest things I had ever seen. I told her about the special box with the magical stars. Then I looked up to her and smiled.

ME: Laura would have loved it.
MUM: Yes, she would. I bet she would have loved it.

As we walked past the bridge, I remembered what Lexi had said about the tablet and at first I wasn't going to but, as we turned down the hill to our road I stopped, took a deep breath and said very quickly.

255

ME: Mum, why do I have to take my 'fit and strong' tablet?

Mum didn't say anything at first. She stopped dead in her tracks and I held my breath. Then she sat down on the bench and when I sat down next to her she tried to explain everything. Lexi had been right. She really did know it all.

MUM: Do you remember when we went to the doctors before Christmas?

I did. It had been fun. I got to have a whole day off school. It was at the hospital where we had been born. I remember the doctor had been really funny. He could do lots of silly animal voices and Rory had especially loved it when he spoke a bit like a duck. Even Mum had said that he was lovely; she said he was 'really nice to look at' and Dad teased her about it all the way home. The waiting room was huge and had piles of magazines, a machine that made drinks and a little telly on the wall. In the corner there was a mountain of wooden toys which Rory had loved and we'd both played with an enormous wooden abacus which had giant multicoloured counters. We had spent ages sliding them back and forth. *Clatter, clatter, clatter.* I'm not sure the other grown ups in the waiting room liked it very much. I remember we had hot chocolate from the machine then Rory and I had X-rays, blood tests and in the end they stuck these things all over our chests.

ME: For the check-up?

Mum took my hand in hers.

MUM: Well, it was a bit more than that. It was because of Laura. They wanted to check to see if our hearts were working properly too.

I suddenly felt afraid. She put her arm around my shoulders.

MUM: Don't worry, we're all fine. We just have to make sure, you know. But sometimes your heart beats a bit quicker than it should.

And as soon as she said it I understood. I understood everything. I understood why Mum asks me lots of weird questions and why she once bent down to listen to my heartbeat.

MUM: We just have to be a little careful. Laura's heart wasn't as strong as yours. But we didn't know. No one knew.

I thought about Laura.

ME: So I just have to take the little tablet then, every day?
MUM: Yes.

ME: Will I be . . . you know?

MUM: You're going to be fine.

ME: Is that why I don't have to do P.E. any more?

Mum nodded. I didn't mind. I hated sports anyway but then I thought of the horrid swimming lesson, how I always got kicked or splashed in the face and how my eyes always stung.

ME: What about swimming?

Mum looked down at me and grinned.

MUM: Nice try, but you need to learn how to swim.

ME: And I won't . . . you know . . . like Laura?

MUM: Your heart is much stronger than hers was.

Even though it sounded a bit scary, I felt better that my mum was telling me the truth and it wasn't as if the tablets were horrid medicine, not like that yucky yellow liquid stuff I had to have when I got the flu, so I didn't really mind taking my little white tablets. I didn't feel ill or sick. I felt just the same as always.

We got up, walked down to our house and at the front door Mum stopped. She bent down to face me.

MUM: So, do you understand? I mean, does it make sense?

I reached out and touched her silver heart locket.

ME: *Everything* makes sense.

I watched a tear run down her cheek, but she was smiling. Then she fished around in her huge handbag, dug out the front door key and as we stepped back inside our little house I started to feel different. I felt something new. I felt as though I had been wearing a really itchy jumper for a very long time. I felt as though I'd been wearing a really itchy, scratchy, jumper and now I wasn't. Now, I was comfortable again.

At bedtime
I lay awake for ages but I wasn't waiting for her. I didn't need to. I just knew. I felt it. I knew she was there. I knew she was near me and she always would be.

VOICE: *Dreams they can be wonderful . . .*
ME: *They are magic in the night . . .*
VOICE: *Where everything is special . . .*
ME: *And beautiful and bright.*

I heard a little giggle and I smiled. I wished all my dreams were wonderful. I wished Laura was still alive too, but somehow it didn't feel as bad as it used to.

26

This year I am having a new birthday. My new birthday will be on July the fifth but don't ask me why, it's a really long story. It's raining today. It's been raining nearly every day for a whole week and I am starting to think that my new birthday will be a very wet and soggy one. Mum has promised me that we will do something exciting but she won't tell me what it is and Lexi won't tell me either. The thing about Lexi is she's really good at keeping secrets and no matter how hard I try, she just won't tell me. I've begged and pleaded but she just lifts her finger to her mouth and pretends to zip it shut. I've tried to guess and catch her out. Cinema? Cinema and a pizza? Cinema, pizza and a fluffy kitten? Cinema, pizza, a fluffy kitten and a sleepover? But she just shakes her head and laughs. I asked my grandpa to come too, but Dad says he'll be in Spain or something. Last night I sent my Aunt Shelly an email to ask if she was going to come, but Mum thinks she has to work. So even though I'm looking forward to my presents, I think that my birthday might just be really disappointing.

<u>Bedtime, Wednesday July the third</u>
   MUM: What are you reading?

I held up my book: *Tom Flemming and The Painted Sky*.

   MUM: Ah, the second book by J.J. Knightly.

I looked down at the name of the author and then Mum took the book out of my hands and sat down on the bed.

   MUM: You know these are really special books, don't you?

She turned the book to the back, opened it and held it up to my face.

   MUM: Have you ever seen this before?

Inside the back cover there was a small black and white photograph of a woman with her hair tied up in a sort of bun. I looked at the photograph again – it looked familiar, but I didn't know why. I hadn't ever really looked in the back pages before so I'd not seen the photograph. I turned to the front cover and looked at the colourful picture of a moonlit sky, a stormy sea and a large sailing boat with billowing sails. A large sailing boat tipping this way and that way. A boat with a name written in golden letters: *The Oberon*.

I'd never noticed that before.

I jumped up out of bed, went over to the bookcase and found the first book. Why hadn't I seen it before? I looked at the cover. There it was again! *The Oberon*. I flipped to the back of the book and saw the same little black and white photograph. Then I remembered, it was the same woman that I'd seen a photograph of on my grandpa's houseboat. The woman with the broach pinned to her blouse. *J K*! The woman with her hair in a bun and two very familiar dimples. I turned back to Mum and held the book up to my face.

ME: Is it?

She laughed.

MUM: What do you think?
ME: Is it Grandpa's mum? Is J.J. Knightly my great-grandmother?
MUM: She is indeed. When I was younger everyone loved her books.

262

I thought about my silly stories, the ones that Laura had loved.

ME: Do you think I could do that, you know – write stories when I'm grown up?

Mum got up from the bed and put her arms around me.

MUM: I think that you could do almost anything you want to.

That night, I had the sort of dream that seems to go on and on for ages. It wasn't the sort of dream that's fuzzy. It didn't keep changing. It was a long dream and it was filled with colour. I was out at sea. I was alone on the magic boat sailing to a faraway island and when I got there, I had to jump off the boat and swim the rest of the way. When I ran up the beach, I found Lexi and Laura. One of them held up a large yellow starfish. They both looked at each other, laughed and Laura said, 'You took your time!'

<u>July the fifth</u>
I didn't want to look out of the window because I'd heard it raining all night but as I slowly opened the curtains I saw that the road was wet, the pavements had puddles but the sky was perfectly blue. Mum, Dad and Rory came into my bedroom singing and tucked under Dad's arm was a large, flat box.

DAD: Happy Birthday, Eddie.

MUM: Happy Birthday.

RORY: Open it! Open it!

As I tore off the wrapping I felt my heart beat quicker and quicker, but when I saw what it was I almost felt my heart skip a beat. It was a computer – my very own 'carry around with you' computer and on the lid in purple and silver letters was my name: Eddie.

We went to Lexi's house for breakfast, but when the shiny black door opened it wasn't Hannah or Lexi. It wasn't anyone I had seen before and when he spoke his voice was really deep and totally different to everyone else's.

MAN: Hello. You must be Eddie. I'm Lexi's dad. Happy Birthday!

He wasn't at all like what I had imagined. He wasn't much taller than Hannah, but he had the biggest tummy I had ever seen and his hair was really long, like a girl's. When he smiled I saw that he had a big gap between his two front teeth and he wore a little earring in his left ear.

MAX: So we're having a picnic. I'm starving! But then again I'm nearly always hungry – Lexi will tell you that!

I giggled and then Rory pushed his way through my legs and we all entered Lexiland.

For breakfast we had the world's most perfect picnic in the secret, hidden garden. Lexi had got the kitten she'd asked for and it was the cutest thing I'd ever seen.

MUM: So, Lexi, what are you going to call him?

Lexi looked over to me and smiled.

LEXI: We haven't decided yet. Have we?
ME: Maybe we could use Hannah's special book?

Lexi lay back on the rug and tucked her hands behind her head. I sat watching her for a little while, but she didn't tell me off. She didn't say anything at all and I didn't say a word either but it was fine. It was a comfortable silence.

ME: Laura had two freckles on the side of her face.

Lexi lifted her hand up and touched the side of her face. I watched as she ran her little finger along the scar.

ME: But I don't. Mum said that when were really tiny little babies it was the only way she could tell us apart. So once I took one of Laura's pens and made two little dots on the side of my face.

Lexi laughed.

LEXI: Will you always have your birthday on July the fifth?

I thought about it for a second and then I lay back on the rug.

ME: I haven't decided yet. I just hated March the first.
LEXI: I hate Christmas.

She turned over on to her stomach and rested her head in her hands.

LEXI: I hate Christmas and I really hate Christmas Eve.

She'd said this before and I sort of knew what she meant because Christmas without Laura didn't feel right. It was weird not waking up together. It was horrible to open lots of presents without her.

ME: Is that because . . .

I didn't dare say any more so I just waited for Lexi to speak instead. It seemed like a whole hour had passed but then she turned to me and when she spoke it was much slower than she normally did and I almost held my breath until she finished.

LEXI: We were at our old house. It was Christmas Eve and the house was full of people. It was a party and everyone was in fancy dress. Dad was dressed like the Grinch and Hannah was Dorothy from *The Wizard of Oz*. She even had a pair of ruby slippers. And the lady who used to look after me, Meena, had made me a cat costume. I was dressed up to look like our old cat, Midnight. I had ears, whiskers and a very long, swishy velvet tail. Meena had even sewn a round white moon shape on to my chest. Just like Midnight.

I got to stay up really late with all the grown ups and watch them doing silly dancing and jumping about, then Dad played the piano and a whole bunch of people started singing really loudly. That's when Meena came to find me and she said that I had to go to bed. But I didn't want to, I wanted to stay and listen to the singing. So I ran off around the crowd of singing grown ups and hid behind the piano. Meena tried to grab me, but I was too quick for her. I went under the piano, through someone's legs and then I made a run for the stairs. I remember thinking that I'd hide in the kitchen and then she wouldn't find me.

There was a woman on the top of the stairs dressed as Alice in Wonderland and I kind of remember her looking at me and smiling up at me but then I raced down the first flight of stairs and . . .

Lexi stopped for second, touched the side of her face again and I could felt my heart beat a little faster.

LEXI: Then my foot got caught on the long, swishy velvet tail. I felt it tug me backwards and I started falling and falling. I remember sort of flying through the air. I tumbled over the stairs. Down and down and down. I went falling and crashing and smashing and . . .

Suddenly Lexi sat up, faced me and spoke in her normal very loud and very fast voice again.

LEXI: And well, I don't remember anything else until I woke up in the hospital!

I gasped and my mouth fell wide open.

LEXI: Dad says it was just as well because there was blood everywhere!

Then Lexi did her *super-fast* talking so I had to concentrate to keep up with her.

LEXI: Anyway. I was, like, completely knocked out. I smashed into this big table and there was a glass bowl of sweets that broke into a million pieces *and* I banged my head so hard that I went . . . I went . . .

She flipped over and shouted over at the others.

LEXI: Dad! Dad!

Max and the others turned to face us.

LEXI   Dad! What's it called again? When you bang your
head and you're . . . you know? Un-something? Un-what?

Max looked at Hannah and smiled.

MAX: Unconscious. Un-con-shuss

Lexi sat up and started talking with her hands too.

LEXI: So I was unconscious. For a really, really long time
and my face was all bashed up and swollen. And well, you
know my eye was like, totally ruined and I had four operations and then I woke up in the hospital but I had . . . I
had . . .

Lexi sighed and shouted again.

LEXI: Dad! Dad! What's it called again? You know, when
you can't remember stuff?

Max laughed.
MAX: Have you forgotten?

This seemed to make everyone laugh.

MAX: Amnesia. Am-nee-shar. You had amnesia.

And so Lexi carried on.

LEXI: Amnesia! That's it! Anyway, I had amnesia and when I woke up I couldn't remember anything. At first, for a few days I didn't even know who Dad was! I kept saying 'Who? What?' It was really weird. I just saw this red-haired grown-up and I was like, 'Who are you?'

Lexi giggled.

ME: You really didn't know?
LEXI: Yeah, for three whole days! And the nurses had to keep telling me, 'This is your mother.' In the end, one of the doctors said, 'Hannah, this is Hannah.' And so now I just call her Hannah. But I'm still not good at remembering things. I still get in a muddle about stuff.

Of course! Poor Lexi! It all made sense! I thought of how Lexi *was* always kind of forgetting things. I thought about the time she seemed to have forgotten how to tie her shoelaces and the time she thought we were having a history lesson when we were in the middle of English. I thought about how I could remember everything and I felt bad.

LEXI: I wish I had your magic memory thing and the way you can do those maths puzzles like you're some kind of human calculator.

I watched Lexi pick one of the little daisies and twirl it between her thumb and forefinger and when she looked up at me I smiled.

ME: I will remember for the both of us.

I turned back to the others; I watched Mum and Dad laughing together, I saw Rory stuff two pancakes in his mouth at once, I breathed in the sweet-smelling perfume from all the pretty pink and white flowers and I smiled. Laura would have loved it. It was a perfect day.

Later, when we went inside Lexi's house, she let Rory wear her old eye patch so he could pretend to be a pirate. I lay on her bed, painted my fingernails with her new gold nail polish and the kitten with no name fell asleep inside one of Hannah's red clogs.

It was almost six o'clock when we all said goodbye, but when we drove home Dad didn't turn down the hill like he was supposed to, he drove across the bridge instead.

ME: Are we going to Grandma's now?
MUM: It's a surprise.

Dad turned left into the park, followed the road down past the woods, past the duck pond and then he stopped by a large wooden gate. My eyes widened when I saw them. I counted six in the next field. There was one shaped like an ice-cream cone and one like a cat, but there was also one which stood out from the rest. I watched as it inflated and grew and grew in size until it was much bigger than the others. It looked exactly like the balloon in Laura's drawing, because it was every colour in the rainbow. Then I saw that someone was standing beside the basket . . . it was Grandpa! He had come! I ran over to him and threw my arms around his waist.

GRANDPA: Surprise! Your hair has grown a bit. You ready to get in?

He hugged Mum, kissed her cheek and I looked at up at the balloon. I heard the loud roar as it was filled with more hot air and I watched as Mum and Dad climbed inside. Dad held out his hand and at first I hesitated, at first I wasn't sure.

ME: Will we go up very high?

Dad smiled down at me.

DAD: You'll be fine, don't worry.
GRANDPA: You're safe, Eddie. Nothing's going to happen. You're going to watch the sunset from the sky.

Rory climbed up on to Grandpa's shoulders and I felt the basket move. It creaked and swayed and as I peered over the edge, I saw the ground move away from us. We were lifting up and up. Grandpa waved and then I remembered the boat, I remembered the name.

ME: GRANDPA!

GRANDPA: YES!

ME: ARE YOU NAMED AFTER THE BOAT? IS OBERON YOUR MIDDLE NAME?

We surged upwards so I couldn't hear him, but I saw him raise his left thumb up to the sky. The basket creaked and it swayed and I watched the fields getting smaller and smaller. I saw the whole of the park and in the distance I could just see the bridge. My stomach flipped over and I felt myself tilting. I started to feel sick and hot and flustery. The basket suddenly surged upwards again and my heart beat much quicker.

ME: I don't like it. I don't like it! Mum, I don't like it.

I sat down in the corner of the basket and Mum bent down to me and cupped my face in her hands.

MUM: Eddie, I need you to help me. We have something important to do, don't we?

She unfastened her rucksack and reached inside. She reached inside and pulled out the urn. But it was different. It wasn't ugly any more; it had been painted. I looked at the colours and I knew it had to have been painted by Hannah – it looked just like the beautiful things in her garden room. Mum handed it to me. It had been painted turquoise in sweeping waves and when I turned it around in my hands, I saw a pair of red lips. Mum laughed.

MUM: That was Aunt Shelly.

There was also a pretty goldfish, three golden stars and a perfect red heart. I touched the red heart with my thumb.

MUM: That was me.

I ran my fingers over the heart. Underneath it was a yellow triangle with three wheels and I laughed.

DAD: That was me.

And on the lid were two very familiar little red hand prints.

MUM: And that was Rory. So what do you think?

I held the urn up to the sunlight.

ME: Laura would love it! I love it! It's perfect!

We flew around the parkland, above the river and I saw the bridge getting nearer and nearer. I could just see the street where I lived and where Lexi lived, my school and the top of the zoo.

And then it was time. Mum held my hand and Dad leant out of the basket and took off the lid. And it was there somewhere high above our home, above the bend in the river and not far from the bridge. It was there high up somewhere that we let Laura go and she was everywhere once more. I felt my mum and dad's arms around my shoulders and I knew that they were smiling too.

ME: Mum, what does my name mean?
MUM: Eddie or the one you crossed out?
ME: The one I crossed out.
MUM: It means whole or complete.

I leant the back of my head against her chest and I felt my hand curl into hers.

ME: Mum?
MUM: Yes?
ME: Sometimes, at night time . . . sometimes I . . . sometimes I talk to Laura.
MUM: I know.

I said nothing else and waited.

MUM: Sometimes . . . sometimes I do too.

I squeezed her hand tightly. Then we all heard shouting from below us and as the balloon hovered above the bridge I saw another crowd of people on the grassy hill behind. Grandma, Max, Hannah, Grandpa, Rory and Aunt Shelly were all there and in their hands they held up a large white banner and painted in multicoloured letters were the words:

HAPPY BIRTHDAY US!

Dad handed me his pocket-sized binoculars and when I looked through them I could see Lexi turning cartwheels in front of the sign and she wasn't wearing her patch. I waved down to her and I could hear her shouting, 'Eddie! Eddie! Eddie!'

The balloon man tapped me on the shoulder and asked me if I wanted to go higher. So as the sun began to set and as we were all bathed in golden light, I leant out of the basket and shouted in my loudest ever voice, 'Up, up and away.'

Epilogue

I died on March the first, which was kind of annoying because it was my birthday. It was our birthday. But don't worry, it didn't hurt or anything and at least I got to open all my presents first.

One day last year when my sister was really cross and sad she cut off all her hair. It was something which seemed funny at the time and it's taken a long time for her hair to grow back. It's taken ages for her sticky-uppy hair to look normal again because for months and months she looked a bit crazy. And even though she can just about get it into a sort of ponytail, it still looks a bit funny.

I'm not sure it will ever be quite the same again.

I think my sister would love to have hair like her new friend Lexi. I think she would love to have beautiful red curls which spring up when you pull them. I used to want golden princess hair like our Aunt Shelly's but when I told my mum she shook her head, stroked

277

my cheek and said, 'Anyone can grow their hair long, cut it, curl it or dye it golden blonde.'

In eight days it will be Christmas Eve. Lexi can't wait because this year isn't going to be any ordinary Christmas – it will be a Canning Circus Christmas. I know! Try saying that three times really quickly.

On Christmas Day, my sister, Grandpa, Grandma, Aunt Shelly (and her new boyfriend), Mum, Dad, Rory, Lexi's aunt and uncle, her cousin Ethan, her nan and grandpa will ALL be going for Christmas lunch at Lexi's house.

My sister might get to play on the beautiful piano again. Rory will probably wear his new pirate costume, Grandma will bake her delicious Christmas cake and Hannah will have decorated the house with the most beautiful handmade Christmas decorations. Dad will probably eat more roast potatoes than anyone else and Mum said that she might even get her favourite dress out again. The one that makes her look like a Christmas bauble.

Last night when Lexi was lying in my old bed she told my sister that this Christmas might just be her bestest ever Christmas.

I might be wrong, but I think that it will be pretty fantastic too.

Acknowledgements

Thank you my lovely husband Alan Moore. I would have messed it up if it hadn't been for you and I write much better stuff because of you x x x

Thank you Alexandra Hemming a wonderful friend whom I cannot live without and who made me smile when I had so many doubts.

Thank you to MBA literary agents and to the gorgeous and very lovely Sophie Gorell Barnes *'a jewel of a person in every single way'*.

Thank you to my amazingly talented editor Jane Griffiths who turned my rough werds into **our** book.

Thank you big brother Jonathan Farber for your patience, kindness and support.

Thank you Bex, Nicola and Penny for reading my stuff and for telling me to keep going even when I can't spell the werds rite and I get the grammerz' all rong.

About the author

SUZI MOORE was brought up in Manchester but now lives in Somerset with her husband. She is well-tuned in to what children like to read, having worked as both a nanny and a teaching assistant. *Lexiland* is Suzi's first young fiction novel, but she has also written a picture book, *Little One's Bedtime*, which published in 2011. She's currently hard at work writing a second young fiction novel.